He   **ut**
him.

He was trim, too, and although the scrubs hung loosely on his lithe frame, she could quite easily see he had well-formed biceps and strong, lean shoulders. Finally, she met his eyes. They locked and held. Megan was a little surprised to find his seemed to be filled with an equal appreciation, and it was only then she realised that while she'd been looking closely at him, he'd been looking closely at her.

Her throat went instantly dry and she felt a blush tinge her cheeks—although this time it wasn't from embarrassment but more from the knowledge that he'd obviously liked what he'd seen. She knew she wasn't beautiful, but when Loughlin looked at her like that she could almost believe that she was.

BACHELOR DADS

Single Doctor… Single Father!

At work they are skilled medical professionals, but at home, as soon as they walk in the door, these eligible bachelors are on full-time fatherhood duty!

These devoted dads still find room in their lives for love…

It takes very special women to win the hearts of these dedicated doctors, and a very special kind of caring to make these single fathers full-time husbands!

SURGEON BOSS,
BACHELOR DAD

BY
LUCY CLARK

◎™ MILLS & BOON®
Pure reading pleasure™

All the characters in this book have no existence outside the imagination of the author, and have no relation whatsoever to anyone bearing the same name or names. They are not even distantly inspired by any individual known or unknown to the author, and all the incidents are pure invention.

First published in Great Britain 2009
Harlequin Mills & Boon Limited,
Eton House, 18-24 Paradise Road, Richmond, Surrey TW9 1SR

© Anne Clark and Peter Clark 2009

ISBN: 978 0 263 86856 2

Set in Times Roman 10 on 12 pt
03-0709-58429

Printed and bound in Spain
by Litografia Rosés, S.A., Barcelona

Lucy Clark is a husband-and-wife writing team. They enjoy taking holidays with their two children, during which they discuss and develop new ideas for their books using the fantastic Australian scenery. They use their daily walks to talk over characterisation and fine details of the wonderful stories they produce, and are avid movie buffs. They live on the edge of a popular wine district in South Australia, and enjoy spending family time together at weekends.

Recent titles by the same author:

A MOTHER FOR HIS TWINS
CHILDREN'S DOCTOR, CHRISTMAS BRIDE
CITY SURGEON, OUTBACK BRIDE
A WEDDING AT LIMESTONE COAST

To DT—My Scottish muse.
Ps 34:17

CHAPTER ONE

MEGAN wasn't happy. Not in the slightest.

She closed her eyes. Said a silent prayer and took three deep breaths. In and out. Just breathe. Relax. Everything would be fine. She was a grown woman. She was a genius, in fact, but unfortunately her genius didn't extend to stupid, unreliable motor vehicles that broke down so often it wasn't funny. Not any more!

Just as a patient could pick up on her mood, she decided to be nice and calm with the car as she opened her eyes and turned the key once more. She relaxed her shoulders. She smiled—even though it looked as though she was really grinding her teeth. The engine stirred. Hope flared. It turned over once. Twice, as though it was desperately trying to splutter to life. She pressed her foot on the accelerator, doing her best to aid its recovery in any way she could.

'Come on. Come on.' She stroked the steering-wheel. Encouraging. 'You can do it. I know you can. Don't give up now.'

Again her ears were met with the whirring of the engine. She may not know anything about cars but from the sounds of things this one was definitely sick and although she was a doctor, a brilliant and reputed general surgeon, unfortunately, she wasn't *that* type of surgeon. When she'd obtained her master's degree in general surgery, two whole years before she was officially supposed to graduate, it hadn't given her licence to perform surgery on *anything* in general!

'Arrrgghh!' Megan stopped turning the key and thumped the steering-wheel in total frustration. So much for the softly-softly approach. All she'd needed was for the car to get her to work this morning. That was all. She didn't care about getting home. She had planned to deal with that later but she had to be at the hospital within the next ten minutes or…

'Wait.' She shook her head. 'There is no "or".' The fact of the matter was, she wouldn't lose her job, her patients would wait and the meeting that was scheduled to start in exactly nine and a half minutes' time would simply be postponed until later in the day. She'd been working in the seaside town of Kiama, south of Sydney, for almost twelve months and it had taken her quite a while to realise that out here the townsfolk were so laid back and relaxed that sometimes she wanted to check them for a pulse.

Personally, though, she hated being late. It was all part of her high-achiever, type-A, top-of-the-stress-range personality and one which she was trying to change before she did some permanent damage to her cardiovascular system. Now, for instance, she had a very tight pain in her chest which was caused purely by stress. Granted, the stress in Kiama was nothing compared to what she'd been through in Sydney but even so, learning to let go, to relax, to control her breathing so the chest pains went away was something she struggled with on a daily basis.

'Time to take a look at my patient,' she said, reaching determinedly beneath the steering-wheel so she could pull the lever to release the bonnet. Climbing from the car, she was still amazed that she'd broken down on the only stretch of road few people seemed to take. It was a short cut between her residence, on a nice secluded hillside and on the main road to town. She'd decided on the short cut today, thinking it was a shorter distance for the car to traverse, and had hoped it would have been able to get her to her destination. Apparently not.

As she looked beneath the bonnet, even though she had no real idea of what she was looking for, she wanted the problem to identify itself quickly. What was it that she could magically poke or prod to get this car started again?

'You can do this.' Megan prodded at something to try and gauge whether it was hot or not. 'You don't need to rely on a man or anyone else to fix things. You can fix them all yourself.' She touched what appeared to be the battery and made sure that all the connections were in place. 'And if you can't fix them, you'll at least figure out a solution. You're an emancipated woman now. You don't need a man to complete you.' Squaring her shoulders after her pep talk, she checked a few more connections, before returning to the driver's side to try her luck once again.

'Come on. Come on!' she urged as the engine whirred again then wheezed to a stop. Megan frowned. It sounded as though something was clogged, like an artery. If she was in surgery right now, she'd be able to figure out the source of the blockage, clamp and excise the offender, then patch her patient back together confident in the belief that they'd make a full recovery. But this wasn't surgery.

She breathed, trying to remain calm. 'You can do this,' she whispered again. Returning to look beneath the bonnet, Megan frowned as she studied the layout of the bits and pieces before her.

'Car trouble?'

Megan was startled at the sound of a man's voice and hit her head on the side of the uplifted car bonnet. 'That would seem obvious,' she declared, rubbing her parietal bone. She turned to face the only other person to have driven along this road today and found herself staring into the smiling face of a man who had the most incredible brown eyes she'd ever seen.

His hair was dark brown and was sticking out in an unruly fashion as though he'd not long woken up and instead of combing it had just raked his fingers through it. His clothes were of the comfortable variety—dark denim jeans and comfortable boots, loose chambray shirt which had clearly not been ironed and was also misbuttoned. She looked over his shoulder and saw his shiny new ute parked a little way down the road from hers. She hadn't even heard another car come along the road and for a moment wondered if he was a mirage.

None of that mattered as he merely edged her aside and bent to study the inner workings of the motor in far more detail than she'd attempted.

'I can do it,' she protested, not wanting to be indebted to anyone else. 'Thank you for stopping but I should be fine.'

'Is that so?' His rich Scottish brogue washed over her and Megan simply raised her eyes brows in interest. 'How exactly?'

She heard the teasing lilt in his voice and was a little surprised at it. It also appeared he was seriously awaiting an answer to his question. 'How?' Her eyes widened for a second, indicating she had no idea, and he had to admire the way she quickly pulled herself together and turned to look at the engine.

'Aye. How?'

'Well, I've already ascertained that it's not the battery.'

'Mmm-hmm.'

'So I intend to work my way methodically through the different sections to eventually discover what is actually wrong.'

She obviously had a decent amount of common sense because that was what most mechanics did. They checked things over, taking their time and figuring things out. 'Good. Good.' He nodded with enthusiasm and Megan could see a small twinkle in his eyes. He was obviously enjoying watching her bluff. 'And then?'

'And then what? And then I'll know what's wrong with my car.'

'Aye, and how do you intend to fix it?'

'Oh. That part I hadn't worked out.'

'You could always call a tow truck and get them out here to tow this magnificent piece of machinery to the nearest mechanic where everything could be put to rights.'

'Exactly. That's exactly what I'll do and the car is hardly magnificent.' Megan had to scoff at that.

'Och, careful lassie. You don't want to hurt the ol' gal's feelings.' He stroked the side panel of the car as he spoke, his tone lowering to a hushed whisper. 'But why would you want to call a mechanic when I can fix it easily for you and get you on your way faster that it would take for the tow truck to arrive in the first place?'

Before Megan could say another word, this Scottish stranger moved alongside her and immediately had his hands all over her engine. Fiddling around, unscrewing things, pulling out long metal sticks which she vaguely remembered her brother once mentioning was how you checked the oil.

Then he started to become more adventurous, sticking his hand down and pulling out tubes, blowing on them before putting them back where they belonged. He unclipped a big round thing in the centre and checked something else in the middle.

Loughlin glanced at the woman hovering beside him, taking in her appearance. She was dressed in a casual but neat suit that screamed 'career woman'. He knew her type. All too well. He'd been married to that type a long time ago and he'd tried to avoid them wherever possible since then. He should have guessed that even out here in Australia, in the middle of a patch of scrubland with one small road going through the centre of it, he'd find a career woman!

Although he did have to admit that the way this particular woman was dressed definitely suited her. The black trousers combined with a cream shirt and black woollen vest certainly highlighted her lovely blonde locks, which were secured at her nape. On any other woman the outfit might look severe but this stranded beauty had the colouring and the figure to carry it off…even if she did appear to be bristling at the way he'd simply taken over.

As far as he was concerned, she was stranded, he was passing by and he knew how to fix this sort of car. He would do his duty as a good Samaritan and hopefully still make it to his appointment relatively on time. When you were the new boy in town, you needed to make friends wherever possible. Loughlin glanced again at the woman beside him and hoped she wasn't indicative of the townsfolk of Kiama. He'd only been in town a few days and had yet to see anything much of the place, or its inhabitants.

He continued to methodically check his way through the various possibilities and his thoroughness impressed Megan. It was how she treated her patients, checking for the obvious causes and symptoms before graduating to the more in-depth tests, if her initial findings gave conflicting results. This stranger was employing a logical and scientific approach, displaying the fact that he actually had a brain and knew how to use it. For that reason, it made Megan less wary of him, which was odd as she didn't usually take kindly to strangers.

'You seem to know what you're doing,' she stated after a few minutes of silence had passed between them.

'Should do. Had me one of these cars in Scotland when I was a laddie. In fact, it was my first car. Temperamental, to be sure, but if you can get the wee bairn to run, och, it's magic.'

'Uh…I take it you're not from around these parts.' She closed her eyes the instant the words were out of her mouth and shook her head. Had she just stated the obvious? She *hated* that. Opening them again, she watched as he angled his head to look at her. His eyes really were the most amazing colour. So rich and deep.

'No but…' he glanced at the beautiful gumtrees around them '…I am hoping to stay for quite some time. It's rather pretty here.'

A small smile touched his lips and she realised he had an almost perfect curve to his mouth but it dipped a little on the right side. His nose was crooked, indicating a break in the past, but even so, it simply added more character to his features. His brown eyes were alive with merriment as though he honestly didn't have a care in the world. Well…good for him. It was nothing to do with her, even if she did experience a slight twinge of envy.

Megan had always wished to have more of a carefree attitude to life, to not mind what other people thought of her, and yet in the past few years of her life that was all she'd done. Sculpted herself into someone she wasn't sure even she recognised. She squared her shoulders and lifted her chin. Not any more.

'You a local?' he asked.

'No. Yes. Well, I guess I am. For the moment.'

'Ambiguous.' He nodded slowly, his intrigue growing. There was a beat of silence before she offered a bit more information.

'I'm originally from Sydney. I've been in Kiama for almost twelve months.' Now, why had she just volunteered that information? He could be an axe-wielding homicidal maniac for all she knew…although her intuition told her that that wasn't the case at all. It was something else that she was learning—not only to listen to but to trust as well, and that was her own instincts.

'Ah. A drifter, eh?' Although by the cut of her clothes, she didn't drift too far from the nearest shopping centre.

'Hardly.'

'Then you're planning on staying in town? Moving permanently to the sunny seaside?'

Megan shrugged. 'I'm not entirely sure. I'm not really looking to get tied down to any one place.'

'Keeping your options open.' He nodded, wondering if she realised her words revealed a lot about her. Problems with her family? Needing to move around? Find herself? Escape? Escape from a bad marriage? Bad husband? His gaze slipped to her hands and he noticed she didn't wear a wedding ring and he couldn't see any faint tan lines either. In fact, apart from the watch on her wrist and a pair of gold studded earrings in her ears, she didn't wear any jewellery at all. Either way, she was more than likely escaping a painful past but, then again, he rationalised, who wasn't? He himself had decided Australia was far enough away from Scotland to try something new.

'I have to say, though, that it is incredibly beautiful here. I can understand why so many people come from the city for the weekend.'

'Our busiest times,' she murmured, thinking of the A and E department in her small hospital.

'Now you definitely sound like a local.' He wondered whether she ran one of the businesses in town. 'Must be good for the economy, though.'

'Undoubtedly.'

'You don't sound too concerned about it.'

'What? The economy in general or the economy in Kiama?'

'Both.'

'You want to have an economic discussion whilst you're fixing my car?'

'Why not? Or you could tell me more about yourself.'

The stranger looked at her with such charm, such delight in his eyes, as though he knew exactly which topic she would choose. She wasn't about to disappoint him.

'Right, then. The economic structure of our country at the moment is something everyone should be concerned with. I mean, the trade deficit is getting more out of proportion every day and, as per usual, the government doesn't seem to be doing anything about it.'

Her statement was met with rich, deep laughter. His eyes twinkled. His lips curved even wider than they had before and his straight white teeth gleamed. He may not be classically handsome but with his lithe build, his messy hair and his mesmerising eyes he was certainly igniting some hidden spark which had been buried deep down inside her.

The knowledge shocked her.

Megan wasn't looking for any type of relationship. Not with this Scotsman, not with anyone. She was polite and courteous to her colleagues, she was nice to her patients and she avoided socialising wherever possible. She'd learned the hard way that she and love didn't mix, that she functioned best when she didn't get too close to people, didn't get too involved in their lives.

The exceptions were her parents, her brother and her brother's family. Keeping to herself had seemed to work during the time she'd spent here in Kiama but she could sometimes feel that the townsfolk were expecting her to settle down, to stay here for another year or two, and the thought of that made the walls feel as though they were closing in once more.

'The economic problems of your country sound the same as the ones back home.' He straightened and rolled his shoulders before jerking a thumb at his ute. 'I just need to get a few tools from my ute and you'll be on your way in no time at all.'

'So you know what's wrong with it, then?'

'Aye.' He winked at her then sauntered over to his ute, Megan's gaze drawn to the swagger of his hips and the leanness of his long legs. She guessed him to be about six feet four—the perfect height to match her five feet ten. Or, at least, she'd always thought that was the perfect height as that had been Calvin's height and she'd fitted perfectly in his arms.

Closing her eyes, she turned her head, blocking out thoughts and visions of Calvin as they swam into her mind. She controlled her thoughts as she always did, turning her mind to the busy day she had ahead of her…if she ever got the chance to get it started. There was ward round, clinic and, above all, a new colleague starting today. The interview process had been rather different from the ones she'd previously taken part in, as the hospital staff were employed by the board of directors.

She'd read through many résumés about six months ago, given her recommendations based on the technical qualifications of each candidate and then the matter had been removed from her hands. Either way, she was glad help had finally arrived and she was looking forward to meeting the new doctor in question…*if* she ever managed to get to the hospital, that was.

'Are you all right?' Loughlin eyed the woman before him critically, noticing the way her eyes snapped open with a hint of fright. 'Sorry. Didn't mean to startle you.'

'I'm fine.'

'You look stressed.'

'Well, wouldn't you be if your car had broken down and you were now late for appointments?'

'I guess… And I promise that I'm working as fast as I possibly can.'

Megan regretted snapping. It was nice that he'd stopped. Nice that he could help her and even though she didn't know him enough to know if she could trust him, it was no reason for rudeness.

'I'm sorry,' she ventured, but he merely waved her words away with a slightly grubby hand. 'I do appreciate your help.'

'I ken that.' He began tinkering again, this time using a spanner to loosen or tighten—she had no idea which—different parts of her engine. 'Are you always this prickly?'

'Prickly?' There was a hint of warning in her tone and Loughlin shook his head.

'Sorry. Must have used the wrong word. Er…I meant…highly strung. Or…er…not relaxed.' He frowned for a moment, noting her expression hadn't changed. 'Am I just digging myself in deeper?'

'Och. Aye.' Her words were said with a hint of annoyance, but she was more annoyed at the way she was responding to this man than what he was saying.

Loughlin couldn't help but really laugh this time. The look on her face said that he had insulted her and to hear her reply as such was more than amusing. 'Are you teasing me?'

'Och, nay.'

'Just as well because we Scotsmen don't take kindly to being teased.' His words were said with a good-natured smile.

'And we Aussies don't take kindly to being insulted.'

'I am sorry,' he said again, his smile settling onto his face. It really did make him look more handsome than she'd previously given him credit for. Such light in his eyes, a brightness to his face.

Megan steeled herself, realising that *his* type were the ones to charm women the world over. Well, he could just forget about charming her with his rich, sexy laugh because she'd become immune to those sorts of charms. No longer was she a blind fool, following and doing what charming men dictated.

'I was only trying to say that you remind me of one of those wee animals you have in your country. The ones with the quills.' He snapped his fingers as though he was trying to remember what they were called.

'Echidnas?'

'Aye. That's the one. They're absolutely gorgeous and cute and yet they've built this little wall around them to protect themselves from predators.'

'Well, if I remind you of one, then perhaps it's because I think you're a predator.'

He paused at that, as though that thought hadn't even occurred to him. 'True. I guess out here on a secluded road, me coming along to try and help you out could be misconstrued into something dark and sinister from a B movie.'

'See?'

'But that's not the case. I assure you, I am an upstanding citizen and a functioning member of society.'

'I only have your word for it,' Megan countered.

'True, but this could also be equally as sinistorial from your end.'

'Sinistorial? Is that a Scottish word?' She was teasing him again…*and* enjoying it. What on earth had got into her?

'Shush. In this scenario, you might have tampered with your car, pretending to be a damsel in distress, and then when I—the knight in shining armour—stop to lend a helping hand, you skelp me over the head with a brick and knock me out.'

'Hmm.' Megan looked at the ground around them, noticing only twigs and dead leaves. 'No bricks.'

'I ken that. I was just giving an example.' He was silent again, concentrating on what he was doing. 'You know, I saw one of those wee echidnas yesterday.' His eyes were alive with excitement. 'My place is not far from here, just up there.' He pointed in the same direction as Megan's house was. The area was surrounded by Australian scrub bushland which backed onto a nature reserve. There were houses scattered here and there, a total of about seven—at least, that was the number of letter-boxes that were all lined up next to each other at the beginning of the access road.

'Really?' Megan had been in this part of New South Wales for just under twelve months and she was yet to see any native Australian animals. 'Where?'

'In my back yard! Can you believe that? Of course, my back yard is absolutely enormous.' He rolled his r's as he spoke and Megan found she was liking more and more the way her rescuer sounded. His accent had a soothing affect on her breathing, calming the stress and tension she usually felt…especially when she was around strangers. He wasn't hard to look at either.

'I was out for a walk,' he continued, 'and heard something rustling in the dried leaves. Next thing I knew, the echidna just waddled out as plain as anything. Smaller than a hedgehog. Its nose is longer, though.'

'And its quills are spikier.'

'Don't you worry, lassie. I ken when to keep my distance.'

Was he talking about her or the mammal?

'In fact, I just stood there in awe and watched it waddle on by, intent on doing what it needed to do.' His grin was wide, his eyes were bright and once again Megan felt her insides churn a little in appreciation. He was becoming more alluring with each passing second.

He angled his head to one side. 'Is that what you're like? Just waddling on? Getting on with your life and not worrying about anyone else—unless you think they mean you harm and then no doubt you'd curl up into your wee protective ball, oozing spikes.'

Megan couldn't help but smile sadly at the picture he painted but she covered it up with her usual briskness. 'First of all, I'd like to point out that I don't waddle but…for the rest of it…' She shrugged. 'Perhaps. We all have built-in defence mechanisms, protective instincts.'

'Aye.' Loughlin thought on her words, knowing what she said was true. He'd had to build his own walls around him, to protect himself and those who he held most precious. He was about to ask her another question when her phone rang. She took it from her waistband, her tone efficient when she answered.

'Yes?' She listened intently. 'Yes, I know. I'm sorry. I had meant to call. I've had car trouble. Sorry. Can we reschedule?' Megan paused, listening. She turned her back and walked a few steps away for a bit of privacy, even though she knew the man could hear every word she said.

'Really? He hasn't turned up either? That's strange. Never mind.' She paused again. 'No. No. It's fine. Someone's stopped to help out and everything should be back under control very soon.' She listened. 'OK. I'll be there when I'm there.' Shaking her head, she rang off.

'The world waiting for you?' he asked.

'Yes.' She paced up and down, her agitation increasing with each step.

'You hate being held up.' It was a statement, not a question.

'Yes. I have people depending on me, needing my time and attention, and instead I'm stuck by the side of the road with a car that won't work.' As she spoke, she felt the tightness in her chest return.

'All right. Well, before you get too scunnered…' he clipped a tube back into place as he spoke '…give it a try now.'

Megan did as he suggested, putting her hand through the open car window and turning the key. The car, with the bonnet still up, jumped forward. 'Oh, I'm sorry,' she called, unable to believe how stupid she'd been as she quickly opened the door, climbed in and took the car out of gear. 'Sorry,' she called again.

'That's all right. I'll take it personally.'

Megan smiled at his words, again liking the way his lilting tones washed over her. Or perhaps she liked the way he was teasing her. She hadn't been teased in…well, she couldn't actually remember the last time someone had joked with her.

'Give it another go,' he called. She did and this time when she turned the key, the engine spluttered to life. Relief flooded through her and gratitude welled up in her chest.

'Thank you!'

'Don't turn it off,' he said before closing the bonnet. 'And try not to stop too long at any red lights.'

'No. Don't want to jinx it.' She pulled her seat belt on and then put her hand out the window as he came to the side of the car. 'Thank you. Thank you. You're a genius.'

He held up his slightly greasy hands. 'I think it's best if we don't shake on it. I'll accept your thanks, though, and state that it was my pleasure. It's been ages since I've had the opportunity to tinker around with an engine. Especially on one of these cars. They're not really as bad as you think.'

'I appreciate everything you've done. Honestly.'

'I believe you.'

And he seemed more than happy to leave it at that but for some reason Megan felt as though she should offer him money or something. Something to repay him for being such a nice, decent man. His actions might even go a long way to helping her to believe chivalry wasn't really dead. 'I'd like to repay you in some way,' she found herself saying. Why was she prolonging things? She had meetings to get to and a day to catch up with.

'Not necessary.'

'But if you hadn't come along—'

'You'd have called a taxi and probably not been as late as you are now.'

'I also would have had to arrange to have the car towed and everything else that goes along with it. So, in essence, I guess you could say you've saved me a lot of money.'

He thought for a moment. 'In that case, I'm free for dinner tonight. You can spend your hard-saved money on me by buying me a meal.'

'Oh.' Dinner? That was the last thing she'd been expecting him to say. 'Uh…all right, then. Dinner.' One meal. It couldn't hurt. He'd been so nice, so decent. 'Where?'

He named a popular restaurant in town and Megan nodded. 'Seven-thirty. I'll see you then,' she called as she put the car into gear. It slid into first more smoothly than it ever had before. The man was a miracle-worker—at least, when it came to cars.

He smiled and waved as she drove off and she couldn't help but watch him in her rear-view mirror until he was out of sight. What a nice man. What a hero. She'd heard stories of people who were classified as heroes, people who had pulled young children from burning buildings, who'd saved people from drowning.

In fact, most rescue workers were bona fide heroes but as far as she was concerned it was the people who went out of their way to help others in a moment of need. *That* was the definition of a hero for her, and until today she'd never actually experienced being aided by a hero.

Well, she'd have her opportunity to thank him again. At seven-thirty. This evening. For dinner. As the realisation that she would be dining with a stranger began to sink in, Megan bit her bottom lip. She was having dinner with a man—a handsome one at that—and she knew nothing about him.

What had she done? Why had she been so stupid? It was so out of character for her. She didn't have dinner with random strangers. In fact, she didn't socialise at all! Regret swamped her, along with a huge serving of vulnerability. She'd agreed to have dinner with a complete stranger. The chest pains returned, along with her mounting anxiety.

She would cancel. That's what she'd do. She'd say that she had made a mistake, that she was grateful but having dinner with him was simply out of the question. Megan slowed the car as she came to a red light and it was then she realised she could do nothing about her intended meeting for that evening as she had no idea what the man's name was! How could she have been so stupid? How could she not have asked his name? How could she make an excuse to cancel when she had no clue how to get in contact with him?

There was nothing else she could do. Her eyes widened with trepidation as the truth swamped her. She'd have to go.

CHAPTER TWO

LOUGHLIN pulled his car into a service station and headed to the toilets so he could wash his hands and make himself more presentable. He'd been due to have his initial meet-and-greet of the hospital and clinical staff at nine-thirty that morning. It was now nearly ten o'clock.

After he'd watched his career woman drive successfully away, he'd called the hospital to let them know he'd be running late and had been told not to stress or worry due to the fact that the hospital director was also running late.

He finished scrubbing his hands clean and ran them through his mop of hair, the wetness from his fingers spiking the ends up a little. It was a messy style but a fashionable one which also meant he didn't need to bother about a regular haircut. He recalled the crew-cut he'd been required to sport when he'd been at grammar school, and on graduation day he'd vowed never to wear his hair that short ever again. And he hadn't.

Besides, Heather had told him that wearing his hair like this made him a cool, hip father and he'd been secretly delighted at his twelve-year-old daughter's words. The thought of Heather made Loughlin's smile fade for a moment. He wished she was here with him. He missed her terribly but, he rationalised, she'd be here in a couple of weeks and it was up to him to get things organised before then. He tucked his shirt in and then realised his buttons were in the wrong holes. Quickly rectifying the situation, he headed back to his car where he pulled on the tie sitting on the passenger seat.

He was doing all of this for Heather. They would be able to have a fresh start here in Australia.

'Two weeks,' he told himself as he checked the Windsor knot of his tie in the rear-view mirror. 'That's not long. Heather will be here with you, where she belongs.'

First, though, he had to get through the first day on the job and as far as first days went, it wasn't shaping up to be the best he'd ever had. Well, at least he'd have company for dinner that evening. Eating alone only made him miss his daughter, his crazy sisters, his whole extended family even more.

He was looking forward to this evening, to seeing his career woman again, to making a friend. He was new to this country and although he considered himself quite a personable guy, he wasn't looking for anything permanent. He'd done permanent in the past and it hadn't worked. Fatherhood was his first priority and everything else came second. Friendships were what he needed and it was definitely easier to get to know people in smaller communities than large cities.

He smiled to himself as he continued on his way to the hospital. His damsel in distress had been chosen as his first friend in Kiama. Lucky her!

'Still no sign of him?' Megan asked Nicole, the clinical nurse consultant. She shrugged into her white coat and picked up her stethoscope, ignoring the mound of paperwork on her desk that was awaiting her attention. The time scheduled for her morning meetings was well and truly over and she had a quick ward round to do—thankfully, she only had seven patients to see—and then it was time to get an already delayed clinic under way.

'He did call. Said he was running late.'

'Well, at least he called.' Megan frowned.

'Which is more than you did,' Nicole pointed out with a good-natured, teasing grin. They'd been working together throughout the year and in a way had become friendly, but Megan had also shied away from socialising with the people she worked with.

It was the way she now lived her life—not socialising with her colleagues—and that had only intensified after what Calvin had done to her. She stopped her thoughts. Calvin and the memories associated with him weren't a part of her life in Kiama. She'd come here to get away from the gossips, the pitying looks, the awkward silences whenever she'd walked into a room. She needed a fresh start and that was exactly what she was in the process of trying to achieve.

'I had car trouble.' Megan's frown instantly lifted as a vision of her knight in shining armour came to mind. 'Thankfully, someone stopped to help me.' As she spoke, she realised she was smiling and was glad Nicole had turned away for a moment. Megan tried to clear her thoughts. She had work to do and didn't need to be thinking about the likes of her soothing Scottish stranger.

'You should get rid of that car,' Nicole continued.

'Hmm.' Megan knew the nurse spoke the truth but she had to confess that on the drive to the hospital the car had been purring like a kitten. Surely there wasn't any reason to get rid of the car now that it was working well. Perhaps she should ask the man's opinion when they had dinner that evening?

That thought brought a fluttering of excited anticipation as well as anxiety. She was going to have dinner with a stranger tonight. Only the fact she was going to be in a restaurant where she knew the owners was what kept her from thinking of standing him up. Besides, it would be bad manners after everything he had done for her, and while she didn't like to socialise, she also wasn't impolite.

'Megan? Megan?' Nicole called her back to earth.

'Huh?' Megan blinked and cleared her thoughts. 'Ward round. Right.'

'Are you all right?' Nicole sounded a little concerned.

'Yes. Why?'

The nurse shrugged. 'I don't know. You just seem a little pre-occupied and, well…more relaxed somehow. I don't know. There's just something different about you this morning.'

Megan's eyes widened at that. Really? She was more relaxed? Oh, no. That meant her knight in Scottish armour really had had an affect on her. Work. She needed to focus on work because when she focused on work, her world would settle back into the even balance she preferred. Work would get her through. It always had and always would.

'Let's go to the ward and get this day started.' She bundled out of the room, not really looking where she was going, and walked slap bang into solid male chest.

Her hands came up automatically to protect herself and she felt warm, firm flesh covered with cotton fabric. A heady scent of spices mixed with earthy tones and a hint of car grease assailed her senses. The man she'd walked into was warm and very close. His own hands had come to rest at her waist, holding her firmly so she didn't topple over, yet the heat that seared her as he touched her sent little shock pulses buzzing throughout her body.

Time slowed. It had never happened to her before. She'd heard other accounts, she'd read about it in books, but she'd never experienced the actual sensation of time appearing to have any effect on what was happening to her. Now, though, as she raised her eyes, slowly lifting her head to see just who it was she'd bumped in to, she instinctively knew before she even looked into his face who it was.

'You.' The word tumbled from her lips as he, in turn, looked down into her upturned face, a wide smile starting to spread over his face.

'We meet again.' His Scottish brogue washed over her and for that instant Megan was rather glad he was still holding onto her or she may well have crumbled to the floor, such was the effect of his deep, rich tones.

'Again?' Nicole's question behind her burst the floating bubble which had encapsulated them. Megan quickly dropped her hands, her fingertips still tingling from the sensations that touching his chest had evoked. She worked hard to ignore them as she shifted slightly backwards so he would have to remove his hands—hands that were so warm, so clever, so full of promise.

As she stepped back, she bumped into the bookcase in the corner of her office. 'Ow.' She rubbed her elbow, feeling more than a little embarrassed.

'Are you all right?' Loughlin reached out a hand to assist her but she quickly shifted away.

'I'm fine.' She made a concentrated effort to pull herself together. 'What are you…?' She stopped, not wanting to sound rude but wanting to know what on earth he was doing here in her hospital. Had he hurt himself? A quick—very quick—glance over him showed her he looked fine. More than fine, but she dismissed that thought the instant it came into her head. He'd tidied himself up a bit, rebuttoning his shirt, tucking it in, and he was now wearing a tie, his mop of hair spiking a bit more than before as though he'd recently run his fingers through it. If anything, he looked even better than the first time she'd laid eyes on him.

'Doing here?' he finished for her.

'Yes.'

'How do you two know each other?' Nicole questioned, still looking from one to the other. 'Did you work together in Sydney?'

'Work together?' Megan's frown was deep.

'Ah…Dr McCloud. I see you managed to find the director's office without a problem,' Anthony, the surgical registrar, said as he came into the room. There were now four people standing within the door space of Megan's office and she was starting to feel a little claustrophobic, especially as Anthony's words were still swimming in the air.

'Dr McCloud?'

'You're the director? Impressive.' Loughlin held out his hand. 'Dr Loughlin McCloud at your service. Although feel free to call me Lochie.' He grinned at Megan as he spoke and once again she felt that warmth spread right through her. Never before had a man affected her like this, to the point where she was once more having mental blanks as to what it was she was supposed to be doing.

'So come on,' Nicole wanted to know. 'How do you two know each other?'

'Er…Dr McCloud stopped and helped me with my car this morning.' So her Scottish stranger had a name. Loughlin. Lochie. She tossed them around in her mind and found they suited him.

'Oh. Wasn't that nice.' Nicole smiled brightly at the man and put out her hand. 'I'm Nicole. CNC for the place. We're all a rather informal bunch here, quite a close-knit community, everyone nice and friendly.'

Megan watched as Loughlin shook hands with Nicole and noticed the extra gleam of pleasure in the nurse's eyes. Was Nicole interested in Loughlin? Probably. The nurse was recently divorced and reputed to be on the prowl for husband number two. At any rate, it didn't concern her except for the fact that Loughlin McCloud now turned out to be a colleague of hers. That meant he was off limits as far as her own personal friendship scale went. Colleagues. Professional friends but nothing more. It also meant she could now cancel their dinner.

'Everyone's friendly, you say?' His lilting tones once more washed over Megan and she now worked harder to ignore the effects they were producing. He'd let go of Nicole's hand but now he leaned a little closer, his eyes alive with that teasing sense Megan had witnessed when they'd been by the side of the road earlier that morning. 'No prickly echidnas, then?'

Nicole laughed, even though Megan could tell she wasn't sure what Loughlin was alluding to. 'None whatsoever,' the CNC assured him. 'We're all as cuddly as koalas and as bouncing as kangaroos.'

'Good to hear. Good to hear.' His gaze settled on Megan as he spoke. It was deep and friendly, as though he was almost challenging her to be cuddly and bouncy rather than prickly and evasive. 'So you're the director.' He nodded slowly. 'That would make you Dr Megan Edwards.'

'Correct.'

Nicole frowned. 'I thought you said you'd met.'

Not wanting to tell the entire story of her morning to her staff, Megan decided it was better to get things moving.

'Ward round, anyone?' With that, she edged passed Loughlin, ensuring their bodies didn't touch in any way, although that didn't stop her from feeling the heat that radiated from the man. It was as though he exuded pheromones, and as they all followed her on the short walk to the ward, she couldn't help but notice how every female Loughlin met seemed to fall instantly beneath his spell. Was it his looks? His accent? His friendliness?

Megan knew she was overreacting, over-thinking and over-analysing and made herself calm down. He *was* just being friendly to his new work colleagues and she shouldn't fault that, she should praise it. If women chose to throw themselves at his feet, that was their problem. Of one thing, though, she was absolutely sure. *She* wasn't going to be one of those women who fluttered their eyelashes at him, who became enraptured by him, or who swooned at the sound of his gorgeously smooth tones. He was a colleague and he was out of bounds.

As they made their way around the patients, Megan realised the round would take far longer than usual given the fact that the patients wanted to stop and chat with the newest addition to the hospital staff—especially Mrs Newbold, who was renowned for being the biggest flirt in the district, even though she was coming close to celebrating her ninetieth birthday.

'I've seen this district grow from nothing,' she wheezed to Loughlin, intermittently lifting the oxygen mask to her mouth and nose to breathe in the lifesaving gas. 'My parents moved here when I was only a small young thing and I've seen good times and bad times.'

'I'll just bet you have and I look forward to hearing quite a few of your yarns while I'm in town. There's nothing like hearing history first hand rather than reading it in book.' Loughlin took Mrs Newbold's hand in his and held it warmly. With his other hand he pressed his fingers to her radial pulse as he paid the woman the attention she deserved. He checked the charts, listened to her chest and continued with his observations, all the while engaging his patient in conversation.

Megan watched in delight as his naturally caring attitude made Mrs Newbold relax. He made little notations on her chart from time to time, recording the necessary information, and when he chuckled at something their elderly patient had said, Megan couldn't help but let the sound wash over her.

As they got ready to move on to their final patient, Mrs Newbold put out a hand and took hold of Megan's. 'I think you've forgotten to do something, deary.'

Megan smiled at her patient and gave the wrinkled hand a little squeeze. 'What's that?'

'You haven't done my tests. Taken my blood pressure and all that stuff.'

Megan's smile broadened as she placed the oxygen mask gently onto Mrs Newbold's face. 'Dr McCloud did your observations today, Mrs Newbold. You're all done. Rest now.'

At Megan's words, the older woman's eyes widened in disbelief. 'No, he didn't.'

'Yes, I did.' His smooth tones filled the air. 'And I have to say you're doing remarkably well for someone who's had a bad bout of bronchiectasis.'

'You did my tests?' She was dumbfounded and the staff couldn't help but smile as Loughlin once more reassured her that he had indeed listened to her chest, checked her blood pressure and pulse. 'I had no idea.' A look of utter devotion crossed Mrs

Newbold's face. 'I like this one, Megan. You'd better see about keeping him here in Kiama. At least as long as I live, at any rate.'

Megan had to admit that she, too, was highly impressed with Loughlin's natural and caring bedside manner. He would, indeed, be an asset to the hospital as well as the general medical services they provided to the community.

'I'll do my best to ensure he stays, Mrs Newbold.' She leaned forward a little but knew Loughlin could hear what she was saying to their patient. 'It appears our new Scottish colleague is a man of many extraordinary talents.' Her remark was made as she remembered the way he'd taken his time methodically and logically with her car. It was almost as though he'd been applying his tender loving care to the mechanical task, and in much the same way he'd charmed Mrs Newbold, interacting with her while making sure she was in the best working order.

'Really?' He raised his eyebrows, his smile wide and pleased. Megan could see that his ego had started to swell.

'Although perhaps we shouldn't discuss such things in front of him,' she said to Mrs Newbold in a stage whisper. 'He is a male after all and you know what type of egos that species tend to sport.'

'Yes, yes. Quite right, girlie.' Mrs Newbold chuckled, which then turned into a coughing fit. Megan quickly repositioned the oxygen mask over the woman's face and told her to take deep breaths. She saw Loughlin move around to the other side of the bed, both of them ready to act quickly if Mrs Newbold's breathing didn't settle as rapidly as it should, but thankfully there was no need. It did smooth and even out and soon the eighty-nine-year-old was relaxing back amongst the pillows, her breathing as normal as could be expected, given her condition.

Nicole stayed with Mrs Newbold as Loughlin and Megan moved on to their last patient. 'You weren't just teasing me again back there, were you?' Loughlin's words were low as he walked close behind Megan. 'You can't possibly have forgotten that we Scots don't take kindly to being teased.'

Megan glanced up at him as she picked up their next patient's chart, her voice was as quiet as his as she spoke. 'Looks as though you'd better start getting used to it.' They finished the rest of the ward round without another personal word spoken between them and when Megan was sitting at the nurses station, writing up her report, Loughlin sidled up next to her.

'So, Dr Edwards. How did I do?'

'Fair.'

'Fair? That's it? That's all I get? And I was trying so hard to impress you as well.'

'You've already impressed me so you can now stop trying.' Her tone was bland and matter-of-fact but he listened to her words, not her tone.

'Really?' He beamed one of his magnificent smiles in her direction and she found it quite difficult to ignore. 'Is that so?' Loughlin raised an eyebrow, then nodded as though this was exactly what he'd wanted to hear. 'I take it this means we're still on for dinner this evening?'

'Listen, Loughlin. About that—'

'You want to cancel,' he stated.

'Yes. Look, I don't think it's a good idea and it's hardly necessary any more.'

'Any more? What's that supposed to mean?'

'It means that now I know you're not a starving artist who's come out to Kiama to paint and suffer for his art, that you don't need me to buy you dinner.'

'You thought I was a starving artist?' He seemed to take her words almost as a compliment.

'Actually, no. That thought hadn't entered my head until just now, but the point is we work together.'

'And you no doubt have a personal rule that prohibits you from sharing dinner with your colleagues.'

'Well…yes. I do.'

'It's a stupid rule, Megan.'

.

'What? It is not.' She turned to face him directly, ready for a debate.

'Aye, of course it is, lassie. I've learned from past experience that as we medics work such long and varied hours, the only other people we really have the time to socialise with are other medics who work long and varied hours. Back home I'd find it difficult to catch up with friends because I was either working when they weren't or vice versa. It's a common and well-known fact. Other hospital staff are also included in this equation,' he added as an afterthought. 'I wouldn't want my new boss to think I was at all discriminating against the nursing staff or the orderlies or cleaners or anyone.'

'I don't think that. I appreciate your argument and agree—in part—but the fact of the matter remains that I think it's best if we cancel our scheduled dinner for this evening. Initially, it was a way of saying thank you for your assistance but I've said thank you at least five or six times and am now of the belief that that will suffice.'

Loughlin thought her words over for a moment, listening to the finality in her tone, and wondered how on earth he was going to talk her around. He eventually decided on the truth…or at least a version of it.

'If you don't have dinner with me, I'll be forced to eat alone.'

'I doubt that,' Megan murmured.

'And that means?'

'If you're lonely, all you have to do is go to the restaurant tonight, sit all alone at a table and before you've been shown a menu, you'll be invited to join someone else's table.'

'It's good to know the people of this community are friendly…well, most of them.' Loughlin looked pointedly at Megan.

'You've already called me prickly once today so you may as well do it again and get it over and done with.'

Loughlin shook his head slowly. 'I don't think you're prickly, Megan, and for the record I'd still be delighted if you'd join me for dinner this evening as we originally planned. It's not a secret rendezvous, it's not espionage. It's just two colleagues, sharing a meal. Nothing more and most certainly nothing to be frightened of.'

Megan looked at him as he spoke, seeing the sincerity in his eyes. She could feel herself capitulating once again, just as she had when he'd offered to take a look at her car, just as she had when she'd agreed to have dinner with him in the first place. He had charm and charisma and she was quickly discovering that she wasn't as immune to it as she'd initially thought.

Due to their delayed start that morning, it was much later than usual when Megan finally switched off the light to her office, closed the door and headed outside to the car park where her sad little car awaited her. She'd been so incredibly busy all day long that she hadn't given it another thought and she'd been planning to get in contact with the local mechanic and get him to come and collect the car while she'd been working. Well, that had been her *initial* plan but with Loughlin having tinkered with it that morning, she was almost willing to put her faith in his ability. Almost.

Would it get her home? Would it conk out and leave her stranded on a deserted road in the dark? Megan hesitated for a moment at the front entrance of the hospital, wondering whether she should leave the car there overnight and call a taxi instead. Then again, she still had to get back into town for her dinner date with Loughlin. *Date?* When had she started thinking of the evening they'd organised as a date?

Honestly. The man had her all in a tizz and she didn't like that at all. Squaring her shoulders and pulling her car keys from her bag, she decided to risk the car and headed out into the cool autumn evening. It was getting close to seven o'clock which meant the sun had well and truly set. Bright lights illuminated the car park and she was grateful for that reserved parking spot of hers very close to the front doors.

She stopped in front of her car and looked at the man who was leaning on the bonnet, obviously waiting for her. He looked very similar to how he'd been when she'd first met him. The tie had disappeared, the top few buttons of his shirt were undone and the shirt had been pulled free from the dark denims he wore. His hair, however, was standing up in even bigger spikes than before, as though he'd not long pushed his hands through the dark brown locks. 'Dr McCloud.'

'Dr Edwards.' He didn't move and her mind started to work nineteen to the dozen to try and figure out what he wanted.

'Why, pray, tell, are you leaning against my car?'

'Well, I thought that, given the late hour and that we are due to be meeting in town in a little over half an hour's time, I'd give you an escort home to ensure that you didn't have any further car trouble. Although…' he patted the bonnet of her car lovingly '…this wee beauty shouldn't give you any more trouble. Not tonight, at least.'

'You'll follow me home? In your car?' She frowned a little, wanting to clarify exactly what he was saying because she was finding that sometimes she tended to listen to the lilt of his words rather than what he was actually saying. She had discovered the more time she spent with Loughlin McCloud that his accent had the most calming effect on her. Stress had always been something she'd battled, given that she was such a perfectionist, and those stress levels had increased somewhat when Calvin had publicly humiliated her. Now, though, the rise and fall of her new colleague's deep voice made her want to sit back, relax and listen to more.

It was a scary shame that his physical nearness created such an opposite effect because being too close to him only brought more tension and stress. Even now she was all too aware of his tall frame as he stood and pulled his own car keys from his pocket. He really was the whole package.

'Aye.'

His one word helped to snap her mind back to attention and as she quickly pondered the scenario, decided it seemed pointless to argue. He was providing an answer to the questions she'd just been asking herself and this way if the car did break down, help would be readily available…sexy, Scottish help. 'OK.'

He raised his eyebrows. 'Just like that?'

'It's a logical solution. Your housing, I'm guessing, has been provided with the job—as was my housing—which would no doubt make us near neighbours so it's not as though I'm taking you out of your way. Also, I now know that you're *not* an axe-wielding homicidal maniac and that I'll be perfectly safe with you.'

He grinned at her words. 'Axe-wielding what?'

'Never mind. Are you ready?'

'Uh…sure. It's just that I was going to convince you of my brilliant plan, that's all.'

'I'm convinced. Your brilliant plan is brilliant.' Her words were spoken matter-of-factly as she unlocked the driver's door, putting her briefcase and handbag into the back seat of the car. She needed to keep things businesslike with Loughlin if she was going to succeed in keeping her distance. She'd been hurt so badly before and although over a year had passed, she was still extremely wary of any involvement with her colleagues beyond the guidelines she'd already set for herself.

'Right, then.' He quickly spun on his heel and walked to his ute, climbing behind the wheel. A few other staff members had exited the hospital and were calling brief goodbyes as they headed to their own cars. 'After you, Director Edwards,' Loughlin said.

Megan turned the key in the ignition and was both stunned and pleased when her little car started the first time without the need of either coaxing or threatening. She reversed and headed out of the hospital grounds, checking her rear-view mirror to see if Loughlin was indeed following her. Sure enough, there he was and she couldn't deny a feeling of relief to know she would at least get home safely this evening. Perhaps he could follow her home from the restaurant, too. Certainly, there wouldn't be any harm in asking him.

As she drove to her place, passing the spot where she'd broken down that morning and where she'd first met the man who seemed to have invaded her life, she began to realise she was actually leading him to her house. That in itself felt strange. She'd not had any male visitors, except for old Alf who came to fix different things around the eco-friendly cottage she lived in.

Of course, her father and brother had insisted on going through the place when she'd first moved in, making sure it was safe for her, but as far as male 'friends' went, she hadn't had any inside her house. Then again, perhaps Loughlin wouldn't come in. Perhaps he would just follow her up her driveway, wave, toot and drive off to his place. If they were going to make the seven-thirty reservation he'd made that afternoon, they'd need to hustle.

Unfortunately, as she turned to go up the last little hill that led to her house, the car started to splutter a bit. 'Oh, no. You were doing so well,' she encouraged. 'Nearly there. Nearly there. Come on. You can do it.' Her words were more pleading than anything else and finally, after literally crawling up the hill, she turned into her fairly long driveway. Once the car had its wheels safely on the driveway, it spluttered again and as though it just couldn't give any more, it conked out. Stopping dead.

'No.' Megan closed her eyes and leaned her head forward onto the steering wheel. She tried the ignition again but this time her efforts were only met with a simple *click* rather than any sort of whirring, indicating that the electrics had indeed died.

When Loughlin knocked on the driver's window, Megan jumped but knew instantly that it was him. She opened the door. 'Put it in neutral and I'll push you up the rest of the way,' he ordered.

'I was thinking of leaving it here.'

'You cannae do that to the car,' he protested. 'At least let it have a good night's rest in the garage.'

Megan gave him a concerned look. 'It's a car, Loughlin.'

'Yes, and as such should be looked after by its owner. Come on. Hop in and do the steering. These things are light and, if nothing else, it'll bring back memories of when I used to have to push mine around the hills of Scotland as a laddie.'

She couldn't help but smile at his words and in that one instant started to feel better. Doing as he had suggested, it didn't take that long for them to get the car to her garage, where she pulled on the handbrake and climbed from the vehicle.

'Right, then, Megan. I'll scamper back to my place, get changed and be back to pick you up in ten minutes.' He pointed a finger at her. 'No more than that so be ready for my return,' he called as he started to jog down her driveway towards his own car, waving as he went.

Megan was left with nothing to do except what he had suggested. No time to overreact, over-think or over-analyse. The last thing she wanted was to have him standing in her living room, waiting for her to finish getting dressed. She managed to have a very quick shower, needing to be refreshed after the day she'd managed to survive, and then stood a whole two minutes in front of her wardrobe, deciding what on earth she should wear.

Usually, she threw on whatever was closest or cleanest but it had been quite some time since she'd had dinner with a man—date or not—and she found the feminine side of her starting to rear its head, demanding she at least look different from how she dressed when she went to work every day.

A dress? A skirt and shirt? High heels? Flat shoes? Make-up? Jewellery? Hairstyle? Too many decisions and not enough time. If she didn't move soon, Loughlin would be on her doorstep in a moment and would find her still standing in her underwear in front of her wardrobe.

That was enough to spur her on and, telling herself she didn't care what he thought, she pulled on a pair of black jeans and a maroon knit top which had decorative beading on the front. She'd bought it on a whim when shopping with her sister-in-law. Jennifer had talked her into it but still Megan wasn't sure if it was really her style. Tonight seemed as good a night to try it out and, besides, she was running out of time. As it was cool, she picked up her dark denim jacket and slipped her feet into a pair of flat and comfortable black shoes.

Thankfully, her blonde hair was cut short, which generally meant she didn't need to style it for work. Now, though, she toyed with it for a whole thirty seconds, trying to decide whether she should clip it back on one side. Or perhaps both? She turned her head from side to side, studying her reflection as she held the strands back. Too dressy? Too much?

Hearing the sound of Loughlin's car coming up her driveway, she stopped dithering and clipped it back, quickly applying some mascara and lip gloss. Her cheeks needed no rouge on them because the simple fact that she was dressing up to go out on a date—no, not a date, dressing to go out for an evening with a colleague, simply to say thank you for his help—was enough to give her cheeks a natural glow all their own.

She heard the driver's door open and close and realised he was on his way to her door. The engine of his car still running, which meant he wasn't going to be waiting around for her to finish primping in front of the mirror.

She grabbed her handbag and headed to the front door, opening it at the same time he raised his hand to knock.

'And we meet again,' he murmured, then stepped back to admire the woman before him. His eyes widened in delight and appreciation. 'Wow!'

CHAPTER THREE

LOUGHLIN stopped still where he was and simply stared at the
woman before him. In one day he'd seen quite a few different
sides to Megan Edwards and this was one he instantly decided
he wouldn't mind seeing more of. 'Director Edwards,' he
drawled. 'You scrub up nicely. Love the top. Very nice.'

Megan wasn't at all sure what to do or say. Loughlin had
changed his jeans and now wore a light blue shirt with a dark
black T-shirt beneath. The shirt, as that morning, wasn't tucked
in and the effect, with his crazy, uncontrollable hair, was quite
intoxicating. And now he was standing there paying her lovely
compliments.

'Ready to go?' he added when it appeared Megan wasn't
about to move.

'Huh? Oh. Yes. Sorry.' She turned around and pulled the door
closed behind her, giving herself a bit of a mental shake and
feeling a little embarrassed that she'd just been standing there
staring at him, not saying a word.

'We'll end up being about five minutes late,' he continued con-
versationally as they walked to his car, Loughlin holding the
door for her.

'Er...thank you.' He was quite the gentleman and in a world
where equal opportunity ruled, it was nice to see that chivalry
was not dead.

'Now, you don't think we ought to call and let the restaurant know we'll be late? I wouldn't want them to give away our reservation,' he added as he climbed into the driver's side and started the engine.

'This isn't Sydney—or Glasgow for that matter, Loughlin. This is Kiama. Sea-change town. People come here from Sydney to kick back, relax and spend time at the beach on the weekends so they can cope with the Monday to Friday daily rut their lives have become.'

Loughlin raised his eyebrows at her words. 'Interesting statements you're making there, lassie.'

'Just observations.' Megan shrugged, wanting to change the subject. She liked it way too much when he called her lassie.

'How long have you been here in this sleepy little sea-change town?'

'Almost a year.'

'And you don't like it?'

'Oh, no. I do like it.'

'But you don't want to stay here. Right?'

Megan tugged her jacket around her as he spoke. For some reason, his words made her feel vulnerable and she hated feeling that way. 'I'm not sure what I want. I just know I need change. Whatever that is.' She had murmured the last part more to herself but Loughlin nodded, indicating he'd heard her.

'Life can sometimes get to the point where it...stagnates.' He nodded.

'You feel the same way?'

'I'm in Australia, Megsy.' He glanced over at her as he spoke but due to the lack of lighting she couldn't make out his features.

'Please don't call me that,' she said softly.

'Why not? It suits you. Makes you seem less...oh, I don't know...prickly?'

Megan merely shrugged at his words, not wanting to get into a debate about it. Although she was classified as having a brilliant mind, it was more to do with work and academic matters. Social interaction was something she'd struggled with all her life which was why she wasn't all that good at making friends, making small talk or having a casual dinner with her colleagues. People needed to persist with her, to dig a little deeper beneath the surface, and then, usually after quite a while, she could let them in. She'd done that with Calvin. She'd let him into her inner sanctum and look how that had turned out. All the barriers she'd spent years learning how to deconstruct had been re-erected when he'd jilted her at the altar.

They were almost in town and within a few more minutes Loughlin had parked the car in the restaurant car park and was coming around to open the door for her. Megan didn't want to wait for him. She needed to become immune to his charm, to show him that she was an independent woman and that she could open her own door. She didn't need a man in her life.

Loughlin merely raised an eyebrow. 'An independent woman.' There was a polite smile on his face and she somehow got the feeling that he didn't approve. Surely a man in this day and age would want a woman who wasn't a leech or a lemming. Surely a man would want a woman who could think for herself, who went after what she wanted, who knew her own mind.

Even though it seemed he was trying to size her up, she had plans to do the same thing to him. Loughlin McCloud intrigued her and she wanted to know more about him. Information such as what had brought him here to Australia in the first place and how long he planned to stay. Those two questions were top of her list. She also knew that being seen together away from the hospital might give the town gossips something new to discuss but she was willing to put up with that if it meant she could start to figure out exactly what Loughlin McCloud wanted from the community, the hospital and from her. Because everyone wanted something. Calvin had taught her that.

'Something wrong?' Loughlin asked after they'd been warmly greeted by Paula, their hostess, and seated.

'No.'

'Then why are you still frowning?'

'I'm frowning?' Megan automatically put her hand up to her forehead in surprise. 'Sorry. Was just thinking about something else.'

'What?'

The question was simple and as such, instead of shrugging away the answer and telling him it was nothing, she decided on the truth. 'Just the fact that we're going to be a hot topic of conversation.'

'Because we've come out to a meal together?'

'Yes.'

'And that bothers you?'

'Not the actual fact that we're having dinner. This place has the best Italian food this side of…well, in the Illawarra district,' she added with a small smile. 'No, I mean because we're together. I mean, out together. Eating together.' It didn't matter which way she said it, even to her own ears it sounded as though they were a hot item. Kiama's latest and greatest. Megan shook her head and saw Loughlin's lips begin to twitch. A real smile. The sort that made him more handsome than he'd first appeared.

'Think this is funny?' she asked.

'I think it's funny listening to you trying to dig yourself out of a hole.' He put his elbows on the table and leaned forward, his chin resting on his hands, his spicy scent encompassing her once more. 'I take it you're uncomfortable with the thought of being talked about, yes?'

'Yes.'

'Let me guess. It's because you've been talked about before?'

Megan visibly bristled at his words and he realised he might be hitting a little too close to the bone. 'Yes.'

'And it wasn't good?'

'No.' The word was said between clenched teeth.

An awkward silence surrounded them for a moment, Loughlin realising he needed to say something to change the subject but at the same time wanting to satisfy his curiosity by asking her more probing questions.

Then again, that wasn't what he was here for. He hadn't suggested dinner so that he could grill the poor woman. No, he'd suggested it so he could not only eat out for a change but also enjoy her company. When you were used to being surrounded by over ten people almost every evening at tea time, it could make a person feel quite sombre and lonely when faced with peace and quiet.

'Do you have any siblings?' The question came rocketing out of Megan's mouth before she could stop it.

Loughlin raised an eyebrow at the question and he could hear in her voice that she was ready to move on with the conversation, to move the focus onto him. He didn't want to disappoint. He, too, had his own skeletons in the closet but wasn't sure if he was ready to confess all to his colleague just yet. 'Four, and they're all sisters.'

'Wow.'

'Yeah. And to add insult to serious injury, they're all older than me.'

Megan toyed with her water glass. 'That probably helps to explain why you feel so at home around women.' Today she had thought he'd flirted with all the women he'd met—herself included—but perhaps it was simply that he knew how to talk to a woman.

'Probably. That, and the fact that my ma was a successful career woman who not only ran her own business but juggled raising five children pretty much on her own.' His eyes turned sad but with acceptance, not regret. 'My father passed away when I was a mere twelve years of age.'

'I'm sorry.' Megan's words were heartfelt. 'That must have been such a difficult time for you, especially at that age. It's when a boy needs his father most of all.'

'Aye.' He nodded and was solemn for a moment before his ever-present grin was back. 'And then I was alone in a house full of women—all older than me and all as bossy as each other. After my dad died, my mother did her best to fill in a lot of gaps that appeared in my life. My sisters were intent on playing football with me and when I was fourteen years old, my oldest sister gave me the best present of all. She got married.'

Megan smiled at the gleam of excitement in his eyes. 'So she moved out and you finally got a room to yourself?'

'No. Well, yes, there was that, but the real reason I loved it was because she gave me a brother-in-law. That's been one of the bonuses of having four sisters. I now have four brilliant brothers-in-law, which is good because all of my sisters were really bad at football.'

She couldn't help but laugh. Oh, yes. He was all ease and friendliness and she was starting to relax. 'Finding the silver lining, eh?'

'You've got to do it, Megan, or else we'll all end up insane.'

Megan smiled. 'True. My brother's wife died when his twin girls were only one but now not only do the girls have a new mother but I have a fantastic sister-in-law.'

'And I think your brother benefits from this arrangement, too,' Loughlin felt compelled to point out.

Megan nodded. 'Oh, yes. Jasper is the happiest I've seen him in a very long time. Jennifer is perfect for him. My parents love her and it's as though she's the missing piece of the family puzzle. We're all very close.'

'That's great to hear. Family is so important. So many people don't realise how important it is. Parenting is the hardest job in the world and it doesn't matter how old your children get, you still need to be there for them.' There was a thread of vehemence in his words and Megan was a little surprised by it. He was talking as though *he* were a parent. Or was it more of the case that he'd been a parent in the past but that something tragic had happened?

It was on the tip of her tongue to ask him about it when a woman two tables over started calling her daughter's name loudly. Megan instantly turned and saw the father hitting the girl, who couldn't have been more than ten or eleven years old, on the back between the shoulder blades. Was the child choking?

'Narissa? Narissa? Stop it,' the mother cautioned, her tone determined but her face deathly pale as the child continued to gasp for air.

'She's choking,' the father said. 'She's not putting this on, Alice. She's choking. She can't breathe.'

The level of hysteria was starting to rise and both Megan and Loughlin were out of their chairs, heading towards the table, before anyone asked.

'Let me see.' Loughlin immediately took over from the father.

'It's Dr Edwards, isn't it? You've got to help my baby.' Alice, the mother, had grasped hold of Megan and was leaning heavily on her.

'I will.' Megan managed to extricate herself from Alice, which wasn't at all easy. Loughlin was assessing the situation.

'She's not choking,' he said, his tone firm yet calm. 'She's having an allergic reaction. Angio-oedema around the mouth, pulse is dropping, bronchioles narrowing.'

'What did she eat?' Megan asked as she spun on her heel and headed for the kitchen.

'Uh…pasta.'

'What sort?' Megan asked, needing more information.

'Uh…' Alice tried to think but it was clear that her mind was elsewhere, and quite rightly so, but Megan needed logical answers if there was any hope of helping Narissa.

'Fettuccine marinara,' Antoinette, the waitress who'd taken their orders, told Megan.

Megan merely nodded as she pushed open the double serving doors to the kitchen. 'Emergency medical kit?'

Antoinette pointed in the direction of a cupboard, her hand shaking a little at the surprise and upheaval currently going on in her parents' restaurant. Megan didn't waste any time and quickly retrieved the kit, opening it up as she walked, searching for what she knew was in there. 'Has Narissa ever eaten seafood before?'

'Uh…' Alice was about to answer when she spotted Loughlin putting Narissa onto the floor in a recumbent position so he could tilt her head back to keep her airway as unobstructed as possible.

'Has she ever had seafood before?' Megan repeated the question as she located the EpiPen which would deliver a sub-cutaneous dose of adrenaline to help relieve the immediate threat of anaphylactic shock.

'No.' It was Narissa's father who answered.

'Has someone called an ambulance?' Megan asked the room in general as she administered the adrenaline, noting the time out loud to Loughlin.

'The ambulance has been called,' their hostess informed them.

'Good. I need a blanket, please. We need to keep her comfort-able.'

'No wheezing present. Airways are opening. Breath sounds in-creasing.' Loughlin had his fingers pressed to Narissa's neck, counting the beats. 'Pulse is settling.' He looked down into the girl's frightened eyes and brushed the hair from her forehead. 'You're going to be just fine. Relax, Narissa. Dr Edwards and I are looking after you and we'll not be letting anything bad happen to you.'

'She's…she's allergic to seafood?' Alice was sitting down at the table, wringing her hands.

'It appears so. We'll need to do some tests but for now I'd like to get her settled in the hospital for the night.'

'She has to go to hospital? But, Dr Edwards, she doesn't like hospitals.'

'We'll take good care of her,' Megan promised, her tone brooking no argument.

Narissa's father came over to place his arms about his wife's shoulders, both of them looking in total shock at their daughter who was, thankfully, no longer gasping for air.

'She's never had seafood before,' Alice was saying, shaking her head. 'I've often suggested she should try it but she never wanted to and even as a baby she wouldn't eat any of it and then tonight she wanted to try it because one of her friends at school loved it and…and…' Alice's words choked on a sob.

'It's all right,' Loughlin soothed the upset mother. 'We were here. We can have Narissa tested and now at least you'll know what to avoid in future.'

'Dr McCloud's right,' Megan reassured Alice, giving her hand a quick squeeze. 'You'll be learning a lot about allergies and allergic reactions and what to do in case of an emergency.'

'You mean…' Alice's eyes widened in horror. 'She could have another one?'

'I mean that knowledge is power, especially in this instance. Narissa's old enough and smart enough to understand the dangers and also how to avoid them in the future.' Megan could hear the sound of the ambulance sirens coming closer. 'We'll get Narissa settled in the hospital, as I said. We'll monitor her throughout the night but the worst is most definitely over.'

'And then you'll start testing?'

'I think we'll give her a few days to recover but, yes, we'll get the skin and allergy testing organised so we can find out if she's allergic to anything else. For now, though,' Megan continued quickly, watching Alice's eyes become even wider, 'we want everyone to get a good night's sleep. We can arrange for one of you to stay with Narissa at the hospital this evening.'

'I'll do it.' The father immediately volunteered, patting his wife's shoulder. Megan saw relief cross Alice's face and realised it was *Alice* who really didn't like hospitals. Hopefully, that meant Narissa would be fine for the night, rather than having an anxiety attack at being kept overnight in hospital. She looked at Loughlin and one brief glance was enough for her to realise that he, too, had seen the relief on Alice's face.

When the ambulance arrived, Loughlin took charge of getting

Narissa organised and into the back of the ambulance, talking to her, telling her what was happening and generally putting her mind at rest.

'He's so good with her,' Alice said as Megan repacked the restaurant's medical kit and handed it back to Antoinette, with thanks.

'Yes. He seems to be very personable as far as the patients are concerned.'

'That's just what we need for our community. I'm sure he'll fit right in,' Alice continued. 'And he's such a good-looking man. Is he single?'

'Er…I believe so.' In fact, it was then Megan realised that he hadn't said anything about being married. She'd simply presumed he *was* single, especially given that he hadn't brought his wife along to dinner tonight…and the fact that he seemed to flirt with every woman he met. Then again, perhaps his wife was more than secure in his love for her and therefore didn't care much about his constant flirting. She headed outside with Alice beside her. 'Did you want to go in the ambulance with Narissa?' Megan needed to get her thoughts back onto a more even keel.

'Oh, no. I'll get Geoff to drive behind the ambulance to the hospital. You can go in the ambulance, Dr Edwards. She'll be better with you along.'

'OK.' Megan stepped into the ambulance. 'How is she doing?' Her question was directed at Loughlin but she looked at Narissa as she spoke, pleased to see the swelling around the mouth had started to decrease and the look of panic had now gone.

'She's doing very well. She's staying calm. Breathing is stable. BP is returning to a more normal level, pulse is back to being strong and regular.'

'Excellent.' Megan smiled at Narissa. 'That's great news. We're almost ready to get you to the hospital so it won't be too much longer.' Megan looked at Loughlin and jerked her head towards the open ambulance doors. 'Can I talk to you for a moment?'

'Sure.' Loughlin stepped out of the ambulance, leaving Narissa in the care of one of the paramedics. 'Problem?'

'Narissa's parents want to follow the ambulance in their car, so either you can go with her and I'll drive your car or vice versa.'

'Right. Well, you go with Narissa and I'll drive.' He glanced back at the pre-teen in the ambulance. 'She's going to be all right.' He nodded as though trying to convince himself and Megan was a little surprised at the self doubt.

'Of course she is. We got to her nice and quick and administered the adrenaline. We'll get her tested and all sorted out.'

Loughlin shook his head again. 'She's so young and what a shock to have had.'

'Yes.' Megan kept watching him closely. 'Loughlin?' He didn't look away from Narissa. 'Lochie? What is it?'

'Narissa.' Loughlin swallowed and turned his head to meet Megan's gaze. 'She's about the same age as Heather.'

'Heather?'

'*My* Heather. My little girl.'

'Your little—'

'My daughter.'

Megan's jaw dropped. He *was* married! He already had a family of his own! 'You…' Why hadn't he said anything sooner? 'You have a *daughter*?'

CHAPTER FOUR

MEGAN monitored Narissa closely once they got her into the high-dependency room. All her signs were at more normal levels and the girl was sleeping peacefully. Geoff had taken Alice home but was planning to come back and sleep on a fold-away bed beside his daughter. Thankfully, there weren't any other patients in the HD room so as far as the nursing staff were concerned, they were more than happy to have Geoff there to support Narissa.

'It's the difference between a big bustling hospital and a wee one,' Loughlin said to one of the nurses as Megan entered the staff tearoom. Had he just been reading her thoughts?

When she'd asked him if he'd had a daughter, even though he'd just told her he did, Loughlin had simply nodded and walked off in the direction of the restaurant. Megan had watched him for a moment before climbing into the back of the ambulance and letting the paramedics know they were ready to leave.

'Do you find that, Megan?' he asked as he sat down to a frothy cup of coffee. She was happy he hadn't called her Megsy in front of the nurse. Although they were informal with each other here at the hospital, the name Megsy—up until she'd met Loughlin—had been a family name. Still, she'd liked the way it sounded, rolling off his tongue, but she wasn't going to let him know that.

Honestly, the man had a voice that could inspire all sorts of wayward thoughts and dreams. The problem was, when it was absorbed by the rest of the package that made up Loughlin McCloud, he became a lethal combination. In short, the man was gorgeous. Hypnotic eyes, smiling lips and even the way he wore his hair in a scruffy, spiky cut made her heart race. He also had a relaxed nonchalance about him which she found soothing to her type-A personality.

Megan managed to pull her thoughts back from the brink of getting lost in thought about the man before her. 'What's that? Not sure what you're talking about.' She headed to the mini espresso machine she'd bought the staff as a present when she'd first arrived here in Kiama. It had been the best thing she could think to do rather than drinking the instant stuff they'd had here before. She made herself a drink, needing to be doing something to distract her thoughts from the track they'd previously been on.

'Getting used to the differences between small and large hospitals. Thirty-eight beds. Thirty-eight beds! I used to see thirty-eight patients on my ward round every morning—or at least it felt that many.' He grinned at her over his big red coffee-mug which had the words I'M A LOVER AT HEART written on it. Megan turned her back to him. She didn't want to be affected by his delicious smile or his twinkling eyes.

She was still getting over the discovery that he had a child. She kept telling herself it was none of her business, and it wasn't. Loughlin McCloud was here to work alongside her as a colleague. That was it. Sure, they lived near each other but she could handle that, too. The hospital had employed him, just as they'd employed her. Her contract would finish in a few months and she'd head somewhere else, and Loughlin would stay here in Kiama. There was nothing more to it than that. If anything, the fact that he was a father would help her maintain her distance. Gorgeous he may be, but he was most definitely out of bounds.

The problem was, though, that in her mind it seemed as though she'd known him a lot longer than she had. She wasn't sure why but where Loughlin was concerned, it was as though they had met before, even though she knew that wasn't possible. She'd never been to Scotland and as far as she knew this was his first time in Australia but, then again, she didn't know that for sure.

They appeared to be on the same wavelength, which was good in a professional capacity but not in a personal one. If she could overcome her ex-fiancé's betrayal, she could quite easily overcome the fleeting, mild attraction she felt towards her new colleague. She could easily reconstruct the few bricks he'd managed to remove from the protective emotional wall that surrounded her.

Colleagues. Business. Nothing more. And to prove that point, she calmly stirred her coffee and answered his question.

'A smaller hospital does take a bit of adjusting to. I've been here for almost a year and some days I still forget I don't have all the resources and staffing I was used to in Sydney. On the other hand, parents like Geoff get to spend the night alongside their children and that provides much peace of mind for everyone, especially the younger patients.'

'Exactly,' Loughlin agreed wholeheartedly.

A patient's buzzer sounded and the nurse stood up. 'I'd better go check that. No doubt it's Mrs Newbold, probably wanting someone to sit with her for a nice evening chat.'

Within a moment Megan found herself alone in the tearoom with Loughlin. 'Narissa settled?'

'She's doing remarkably well.'

'Good. Prompt service with a smile, that's what we provided tonight, Dr Edwards.'

Megan nodded but took a sip of her drink instead of saying anything else. He didn't say anything either, obviously enjoying his own coffee. She felt the atmosphere in the room start to become a little bit strained, although when she looked at Loughlin to see if he was looking anywhere but at her, she found he had a frothy milk moustache on his top lip and she couldn't help but smile.

'What?'

'You, uh…' She pointed to her upper lip.

'What?'

He obviously didn't understand her. 'You have, uh…' Megan cleared her throat, her smile growing wider. It was like telling someone you'd only just met that they had spinach in their teeth or that their shirt buttons were out of alignment—which, she recalled, his had been that morning. 'You have a little milk moustache.'

'Oh?' Loughlin's eyes were twinkling at her as his tongue slowly snaked out and licked the froth from his lip. 'Thanks. Wouldn't want to look like a right twit in front of my new colleagues, now, eh?'

Megan's only answer was to smile stupidly at him and try harder to ignore the way her heart rate had increased when he'd licked the froth away. He really was sexy.

He could be married, she quickly reminded herself. He had a daughter and she had no right to be thinking of him in this way. She forced herself to look away. 'You about ready to leave? If not, I can always call for a taxi to take me home.'

'In a hurry?' He didn't move but his eyes were watching her intently.

'No. No,' she quickly denied. 'It's just been a very full day and there are still some things I need to get done.'

'Right, then. We'd best see about getting you home then, young Megsy.'

'Please, don't call me that,' she said, repeating the request she'd made the last time he'd called her by the nickname.

'You don't like it?'

'It's not that.'

'Then what?' He watched her for a moment then nodded. 'Or is it that you don't like *me* saying it?'

Quite the contrary, she wanted to say, but knew she wouldn't. She wasn't the sort of woman who said those sorts of things to a man, especially to a man she hardly knew. 'It's a family name.'

'Family as in parents?' He was fishing and he wondered if

she'd pick up on it. He knew she wasn't married because Nicole had mentioned it earlier on that day. That was another thing about small hospitals, everyone knew everyone else's business. However, if the nickname was from a past relationship, he could understand why she might not want him to use it.

'Yes, and Jasper.' She thought of Jasper. 'Actually, mostly Jasper.' Her tone was one of amused familiarity.

'You never told me before. Is Jasper older?'

'Yes.'

'Ah… I see you know what it's like to be the youngest.'

'Yes, but thankfully I didn't have to put up with four older brothers, as you had to put up with four older sisters.' Her smiled widened at the thought. She could imagine a little Loughlin being bossed about by sisters, being dragged into dress and shoe shops. 'It must have taught you a lot of patience.'

'Och, aye, and when I was about six, we lived in a house with one bathroom.' He rolled his eyes and Megan's smile increased.

'Well, if that didn't teach you patience, then I don't know what will.'

'Aye.' He chuckled and the sound washed over her, making her want to hear more. Which was wrong, but right at this moment she pushed the thought to the side. 'So, your brother Jasper, what does he do?'

'He's an orthopaedic surgeon in Parramatta. So is his wife.'

'And you said he has twin girls?'

'Yes. They're absolutely delicious. Lilly and Lola.'

'Identical?'

'Yes, but completely different in personality.'

'You don't get them confused?'

'Rarely. They may look the same but they're both very individual.'

'Most twins are. You know what it's like to be an aunty, to hype the children up on lots of sugar and then hand them back to the parents.'

Megan couldn't help but laugh. 'Yes. I have done that once or twice come to think of it.'

Did she have any idea how beautiful she looked when she laughed like that? When she relaxed and let her guard down? Let her true self shine through? 'I used to do that to my nieces and nephews. Hype them up and then drop them home.'

'The perfect uncle.'

'Aye, and my sisters delighted in doing the same thing after Heather was born. Still do, in fact. They're always spoiling her or hyping her up on sugar.' He shook his head, amusement dancing on his lips.

'Are you married?' The question blurted from her lips, surprising both of them—Megan most. She clapped a hand over her mouth as though trying to take it back. 'I'm sorry, Loughlin. You don't need to answer that. Ignore me.'

'No.'

'Well, just forget what I said, then.'

'No, I meant that, no, I'm not married. I am, however, divorced. Quite a nasty one actually so I'm more than glad to be on the opposite side of the world from my ex-viper…er, I mean ex-wife.'

'My goodness. What on earth happened?' Again, it was as though her mouth had a mind of its own and she put her hand to her lips once more. 'Sorry, again. It's really none of my business.'

'You're obviously curious so why don't we go and check on Narissa and I'll enlighten you on the topic of my horrible experiences with matrimony whilst we head home, eh?'

'Loughlin, you shouldn't feel pressu—'

'Hey.' He stood and leaned across the table, placing a finger over her lips, effectively silencing her. The touch of his skin against hers and in such an intimate fashion, in such a confined and deserted tearoom save the two of them, caused Megan's heart to beat out a wild and excited rhythm in her chest. This was utterly ridiculous. She didn't even know this man so how on earth could his nearness evoke such an overwhelmingly powerful reaction?

'I'm more than happy to tell you on the way home.' His gaze flicked down to her lips for a split second as though he was tempted to remove his finger and place his mouth there instead. The simple look had heat flooding through Megan's body, her breathing becoming even more shallow. He looked into her eyes once more and she saw that there was a spark of awareness in the dark depths. 'After all, this is a small hospital and I doubt you're the only one who's curious. Better to get the story out there and circulating so it can die a natural death sooner rather than later.'

His tone was soft, his words even and his scent was starting to blend with her own, making a heady combination. Once he'd spoken, he didn't automatically move away and the awareness between them seemed to triple in an instant. What on earth did this mean? Megan's logical mind was trying to decipher the signals, trying to figure everything out so she could understand how on earth she could be so attracted to a man she'd only just met. The only problem was, her mind didn't seem to be functioning too well at the moment.

'Right,' she said, although if he'd asked her what she was agreeing to, she couldn't have told him for all the tea in China. A patient buzzer, which could be heard loud and clear from the tearoom, went off and it gave them enough of a start for both doctors to move apart. Loughlin's hand dropped back to his side, the two of them staring at each other as though they weren't quite sure what had just transpired.

'Narissa.' Megan stood and carried her cup to the sink. 'We need to check on—'

'Narissa,' he finished. It was enough to make them focus their thoughts and go and check on their young patient. After they'd done that and Night Sister had assured them that everything else was running like a well-oiled machine, Megan and Loughlin headed outside into the now rather cool April evening.

'Well, tonight didn't go exactly as planned,' she said as Loughlin drove through town.

'And you still owe me dinner,' he pointed out.

Megan wasn't sure she could go through another evening sitting across the table from him, staring into those brown eyes of his. The colour was so rich, so deep, and his gaze so…probing. When he looked at her as he just had, it was as though he was trying to look into her soul, trying to find out exactly what it was that made her tick. Megan wasn't used to such attention, and hardly knew how to react. Being out with Loughlin tonight had made her feel extremely vulnerable and that was an emotion she was more than willing to avoid wherever possible.

'Are you sure we can't just call it even?'

'Even? I ended up paying for dinner!'

'What? But we never received the food.'

'Well, when I say "paying", I actually meant "collecting". Paula was so grateful for our help she said tonight's meals were on the house and Antoinette had put them into take-away containers.' He jerked his thumb in the direction of his back seat and it was then Megan saw a small box that held two food containers and another package wrapped in foil. 'Paula was worried we didn't get to eat and the food had already been cooked so she made me take it. We can heat it up when we get back to your place.'

'But—'

'Or mine, if you don't want to eat at your house, although I should warn you that I don't have a lot of furniture as yet. Thought I'd wait for Heather to come so we could pick it out together. You know, sort of make it *our* home, rather than just mine.'

'So you're definitely planning on staying?' If his daughter was coming, that sounded as though it was pretty permanent.

'For as long as your country will have me.'

That was interesting news. Although why she should find it so was still a dilemma. 'And your daughter? Heather? Will she stay, too?'

'Most certainly. I have sole custody.'

'Why didn't she come with you?'

'I wanted to get established first. You know, get to know my way around, get settled with work, check out the people to see if they're nice.' He grinned at her. 'That sort of thing. Much easier for her to arrive once I've had time to do all the hard work such as finding a place to live.'

'The job came with accommodation provided,' she felt compelled to point out.

'Shh. Buy a car that works, unlike some other doctors in town that I know.'

'Hey. I hardly think that—'

'And look for suitable schools,' he continued, cutting her off.

'But not buy furniture.'

'Nay. Thought it might be loads of fun to choose it all with my wee bairn.'

'I thought you said she was around Narissa's age.'

'Aye.' He chuckled. 'She's twelve, but to me, she'll always be daddy's little girl.'

'And what about Heather's mother?'

'Mother in name only,' he scoffed. 'Bonnie doesn't care about Heather. She never has. Always find out if the person you're marrying wants children *before* you marry them.'

'Good advice,' Megan agreed, thinking of how Calvin had been nonchalant on the subject of children, whilst she'd always craved a brood of her own.

'In my defence, though, I will say that when I married her I was young and highly immature and Bonnie was very beautiful.'

'I can imagine.' Megan looked out the window but she couldn't see much as he turned off the main road onto the short cut that led to their houses. She could well picture him with a beautiful woman draped on his arm who would undoubtedly be smiling indulgently at him. He was a handsome man and handsome men were always surrounded by beautiful women.

As far as she was concerned, she would hardly describe herself as beautiful. Sure, she was blonde and blue-eyed with a slim frame, but not stunning or anything like that. She'd never had men lining up to date her and she'd come to terms with that. In school, she'd been the freaky genius kid who'd only captured the interest of the opposite sex when they'd wanted help with their homework. 'Were you married long?'

'Eight years. Isn't it funny how you can marry a person and then a few years later you wake up to find yourself married to a total stranger.'

'What went wrong, do you think?'

'Work. I was always studying. Always busy at the hospital.' He shrugged. 'It's not an uncommon story. It's why medics usually marry medics. Bonnie worked as a photographer. We met when the hospital held a bachelor auction and all the men got raffled off for charity. She was hired to take the publicity photographs and let's just say she managed to outbid quite a number of women to win me.'

'Sounds impressive.'

'It was, at the time. Anyway, we knew we were a wrong fit but we didn't seem to care. You tell yourself a lot of lies when you're young, thinking you can take on the world…or at least Glasgow.' He sighed heavily. 'Nay. It doesn't work. Anyway, I was at the hospital for long hours, Bonnie's career started taking off and she was getting bookings for London and Paris fashion shows. Then she discovered she was pregnant with Heather.'

Loughlin pulled the car into Megan's driveway and switched off the engine. He undid his seat belt and turned to face her. 'She didn't want the baby. I begged her to keep it. She eventually conceded. I cut back on my hours, had my sisters and mother at the ready to provide help, but nothing I did seemed to make any difference. When Heather was three, Bonnie walked out. She'd had enough.'

'So does Heather see her at all?'

'Very occasionally. When Bonnie's schedule permits it. Career first…family way, way down the other end of the list.' He shook his head sadly. 'That's my ex-wife.' He tugged at his shirt collar, even though it wasn't tight.

'And when is Heather due to arrive?'

'Two weeks' time.'

'You're going to live with no furniture for two weeks?'

'Barely any furniture.' He grinned at her as he climbed from the car then opened a door and removed the box containing their dinner. Megan didn't wait for him to open her door and quickly stepped from the car, going over to unlock her front door. She knew a lot of people out here didn't bother locking their doors and she guessed that the only houses on this side of the hill were really her own and Loughlin's, but it was still a lifelong habit of hers from living in a big city and it wasn't one she was about to forgo…especially as she was planning to leave Kiama when her contract was up.

'Barely any furniture. What does that mean, exactly?' She switched on lights and headed for the kitchen, picking up a few odd tissues and a coffee-mug she'd put on the table as she'd rushed out the door that morning. As Loughlin came in with the food, she quickly closed her bedroom door lest he should see the mound of clothes on her bed which she'd quickly gone through when trying to choose something to wear out to dinner with him.

'I have a mattress to sleep on. A bean-bag and a card table. What more does a man need?' He came into the kitchen and noticed the mound of dishes in the sink. He grinned, sort of pleased to find that Megan wasn't a complete Miss Hospital Corners. He liked women who were real, who made mistakes and learned from them, who became stronger from those mistakes. He liked women who had self-confidence, who obviously weren't afraid to speak their minds and who didn't care if a man came into their kitchen and found a week's worth of dirty dishes in the sink. It showed they were human…unlike Bonnie.

He tried not to huff with annoyance at the thought of his ex-wife, who had definitely been little Miss Perfect in every way, shape and form—except when it came to motherhood. Then her true colours had shone through and Loughlin had realised he'd been completely duped by the woman he'd thought he'd married.

'How about a bed for your daughter?'

Megan's words brought him back to reality and he stared at her for a moment, trying to remember what they'd previously been discussing. Furniture. A bed for his daughter? His eyes widened as her words sank in. 'Ah.'

'It's all well and good saying you want her here to choose the furniture with you but I think she'd appreciate not having to sleep on the floorboards, at least for her first night in a foreign country after flying halfway round the world.'

Loughlin nodded slowly. 'You may just have a point there, Megsy.' He watched as she took the food from the containers and heated it up in the microwave, secretly pleased she hadn't said anything about him using her nickname. 'So what are you doing tomorrow?'

Megan frowned at him, busying herself by pulling out glasses and cutlery and carrying them through to the dining room alcove. Loughlin followed her, watching her set the table as she spoke. 'I'm going to work. Like you. Tuesdays are usually quite busy thanks to morning clinic and then I have a surgical list in the afternoon.'

'Right. What about after the list is finished? What are you doing then?'

'Why?' She returned to the kitchen and opened her refrigerator. 'Looks as though we'll be drinking water. Sorry. It's all I have.'

Loughlin peered into her fridge. 'Megsy, darlin'. It's a little sad to see a doctor who's well versed in the dos and don'ts of nutrition to have such an empty fridge as yours.' He picked up a carton of milk and smelt it, grimacing before he put it back. 'Doing some experiments? I may not have furniture but at least I have food. Right. We'll go shopping for groceries after we've bought Heather a bed.'

'What?' Megan was stunned at his words. 'Shopping?' The

microwave beeped but she didn't move. Loughlin took the tea-towel she'd left on the bench and removed the glass dishes from the microwave, carrying them to the table. 'I'm not going shopping with you.'

'Of course you are, lassie. You're coming with me to get Heather a bed. I can't very well pick out something for a twelve-year-old girl by myself. I still thought she played with dolls until I found her drooling over a large poster of a male singer. I may be her da' but I still want her to be daddy's little girl and she, apparently, wants to grow up.'

'But I don't even know her.'

'But you're a girl. That's an advantage you have over me.'

'Loughlin, I hardly think that—'

'I'll not be taking no for an answer, Megsy, and if you really want me to pull out all the stops, I'll simply say that if you come shopping with me tomorrow evening after your surgical list we'll call it even with me helping you out with your car.'

'We don't have to have dinner together again?'

Loughlin sat down at the table opposite her. 'Don't say it as though it was going to be torture for you. How is a man supposed to feel when his neighbour and colleague doesn't want to spend any time with him? What sort of friend are you?'

'A prickly one,' she answered with a grin, before digging into her dinner.

CHAPTER FIVE

LOUGHLIN lay on his mattress that night and thought about the day he'd just had. As far as first days went, it had pretty much been one of the best ones he'd had and he knew it was because of Megan Edwards.

She was a woman who intrigued him and he hadn't met anyone like her for a very long time. For years since his divorce he'd kept his distance from any sort of real dating, usually discovering the women were as shallow as his ex-wife. Three dates was all it usually took. He'd developed a skill for asking the right sort of questions to prompt the answers he was looking for. When the wrong answers came—he took that as his cue to leave.

Besides, Heather was his first priority and that hadn't changed from the minute she'd been born. Establishing a solid home life for his daughter was paramount and it was also impossible to achieve with a different woman in tow every so often.

So he'd put dating on the back burner, but that had been when Heather had been little. Lately, though, Heather was becoming embarrassed when he tried to kiss her goodbye when he dropped her off at school. It was evidence that she was growing up. His sisters had pointed it out, telling him he was coming to the time where he also needed to think about *his* needs. Having this distance from Heather, being here in Australia—on the other side of the world—Lochie wondered whether his sisters might be right. It was strange being without Heather but at the same time he was also enjoying it. He was starting to think it might actually be time to find where on earth he'd put his *own* life.

His sisters had often told him he was a good catch, that any woman would be thrilled to have him in their life, but the truth of the matter was that Bonnie had done a right royal number on him and he didn't want to get hurt like that ever again. *If* he thought about dating, about trying to develop more than a friendship with someone, she would need to be one extraordinary woman.

After less than twenty-four hours since first meeting Megan, he'd found himself wanting to get to know her better. He'd flirted with her this morning. He'd been aware of it, even if she hadn't. He'd flirted with her at the hospital and then later when they'd been out at the restaurant. She intrigued him, fascinated him, and, like a specimen beneath a microscope, he was definitely interested to see what she'd do next.

Usually, he never talked about his own divorce, preferring not to think of the failure he'd made of his marriage, but when she'd asked him about it, he'd discovered that he didn't mind her knowing. What he'd said about small hospitals was true but by the same token he'd been more than a little bit pleased that she was interested enough in *him* to ask in the first place.

Of course, he'd just given her the facts, hoping she wouldn't see how deep Bonnie's betrayal had cut him. Still, rehashing old wounds had made him rather exhausted and as he tried to relax again, a vision of the woman he'd spent most of the day with swam before him.

Opening his eyes again, he knew he needed to stop thinking about Megan. It wasn't why he'd come to Australia. He'd come here because he'd realised his life had become stuck in a rut. He'd just turned forty-one and not long after his birthday he'd come to the conclusion that his life held no surprises at all. He knew where he was supposed to be at every given moment on any given day. And that wasn't who he wanted to be.

The job in Australia had been advertised and Heather had been keen so he'd decided to take a giant leap outside his daily grind and do something different.

'And today was something different.' He smiled to himself and switched on the light, reaching for the latest surgical journal, which was on the floor beside the mattress. It seemed sleep was evading him tonight so he may as well catch up on his reading. Five minutes later he sat up and looked more closely at the name at the top of the article he was about to read.

'Dr Megan I Edwards. M.B.B.S., (Hons), M.D., Ph.D, F.R.A.C.S.' He picked up another journal in the pile and scanned the articles, finding another two written by her. He quickly read all three, his eyebrows rising in astonishment and appreciation at what his new colleague had written. Lochie wondered what else she'd written and whether or not, over the years, he'd read other articles by Dr Megan I Edwards. He located his laptop and logged onto the internet to explore this avenue further.

The next morning, Megan was up earlier than usual, doing her breathing exercises and trying to get her stress level under control. She hadn't been able to sleep all that well, especially given the fact that Loughlin had offered to drive her to work. At the time it had seemed churlish to refuse but she'd spent half the night thinking about it, about what topics of conversation they might have, whether he'd talk further about his daughter or his life back in Scotland.

It was a country she'd often wanted to visit but never had. In fact, there was a lot she'd wanted to do in life but hadn't. There had always been something holding her back…her age, her study, her job, Calvin. Of course she'd travelled but it had always been for work purposes. However, she'd never visited Scotland and now that she'd met Loughlin, she was interested to know more.

She was outside her now tidier house, waiting for Loughlin's ute to head up her driveway. When it did and she saw him behind the wheel, a smile spread across her face. She couldn't help it. She didn't want to be happy to see him, yet she was. Spending time with him yesterday had almost been a wake-up call for her.

To her utter astonishment, she'd found herself not only interested in getting to know a colleague a bit better but that she acknowledged she was attracted to him. Then again, she rationalised, every woman in the town was attracted to him, whether they were old or young, married or single. Given that that was the case, it actually made Megan feel as though she was normal.

'First time for everything,' she muttered as she walked over to the ute when Loughlin brought it to a halt. Forcing herself to relax, or at least appear relaxed, she climbed in. She had her list of conversation topics all neatly outlined in her mind, what subjects would be suitable and which ones would not. She wouldn't let him sweet talk her or charm her and even if he did try, she would remain immune. She was a strong woman, in control of her life, and no gorgeous Scottish knight in a shiny ute was going to swoop her off her feet.

'Top of the morning to ya.' His smile wide and welcoming. Good Lord. She nearly faltered right then and there in her resolution. Megan angled her head to the side.

'I thought you were from Scotland. Not Ireland.'

'What? You think the Irish have the monopoly on morning greetings?' He tut-tutted and shook his head. 'You need to get out more, Dr Megan I Edwards.'

She gave him a puzzled look. 'Sorry?'

'I've been reading about you or should I say I've been reading your papers. You're extensively published, Dr Megan I Edwards. I'm highly impressed and a little in awe.'

It was the last thing Megan had been expecting him to say and it definitely wasn't on her mental list of acceptable topics. 'Er…thank you, I guess.' Why did his words, the way his deep tones washed over her…why did they have to be so charming?

'There's just one thing that's now been driving me a wee bit insane for the past eight or so hours.'

'And what is that?' she prompted when he didn't speak straight away.

'What does the "I" stand for? There aren't that many girl's names that begin with the letter "I" and I've been racking my brains trying to come up with as many as I can. Irene, perhaps?'

Megan smiled at the way his r's had rolled as he'd spoken and she took a deep breath into her lungs, filling them quite deeply for a change, before slowly exhaling. His voice really did have such a soothing effect. When she'd been living in Sydney, she'd struggled to take deep breaths without getting the occasional twinge of chest pain. She hadn't wanted to see anyone about it given the fact that Calvin had been head of cardiology and had connections everywhere. The pains had become far worse after he'd jilted her, which was to be expected. She'd hoped that the more sedate pace of life in Kiama would help reduce her stress and whilst it had, breathing deeply without a hint of pain had been unachievable until she'd met Loughlin. Yes, Loughlin's drawl definitely had a soothing effect on her equilibrium…or was it simply *Loughlin* as a whole who had that effect? He certainly was an enigmatic man and he was expecting an answer to his question.

'Er…well, it's no big secret. It stands for Iris. It's my mother's name.'

'Iris.' He rolled the word over in his mouth. 'You know, that was one I didn't even think of. It's beautiful.'

She was touched by his words. 'Thank you, Lochie. I'll tell my mother you said so.'

'You do that.' He smiled as he continued the drive to the hospital, once more secretly pleased that she seemed to be mellowing towards him by calling him Lochie. He liked the way his nickname sounded coming from her lips…and he probably shouldn't. In reading her articles, he'd already started falling for her mind, such was the level of her intelligence. It wouldn't do to enhance the fascination any further by liking the way she said his name.

They were colleagues. Neighbours. Friends. Nothing more.

When they arrived at the hospital, Megan discovered that another patient had been added to her afternoon list. She spoke to Anthony, her surgical registrar, about it and reviewed the patient who'd been admitted to the ward and was currently fasting.

'I'll have to do him last,' Megan said to Anthony as Loughlin came into the tearoom. 'It means the list will run late, though.'

'We could bump Mr Johns.'

'No. He's been waiting too long. We'll just run overtime and leave it at that.'

'Problems?' Loughlin asked.

'Just list juggling. Have an extra cholysystectomy added to the list. Not sure what time we'll be finished.'

'Happens.' He shrugged his shoulders, not seeming too bothered. Had he remembered that he'd all but insisted she accompany him on his little shopping trip that afternoon? Secretly, she'd actually been looking forward to it. Buying a bed was a special experience and she saw it as a challenge to be helping Loughlin purchase one for a twelve-year-old girl, especially a girl she was yet to meet. It had nothing to do with spending more time with Loughlin. Nothing at all.

'Anyway, let's get the morning clinic started so that we don't run even further overtime this afternoon.' She turned on her heel and walked from the room, still holding her coffee. She'd told herself to keep things strictly professional with Loughlin even though he seemed to be taking huge chunks out of the protective wall she'd built around herself. He was here to work. So was she and that's what they would do.

Clinic was as hectic as she'd predicted and a ten-minute break was all she had time for before her list was due to begin.

'There you are.' Anthony came bursting into the tearoom. 'What's the matter?' He was puffing and took a moment to catch his breath.

'It's Romana. She's gone into labour.'

Megan's eyebrows hit her hairline as she quickly finished her yoghurt. Romana was Anthony's wife and she was on the hospital staff. 'Where is she? Is she here? She's only—what?—twenty-nine weeks?'

'Twenty-eight,' Anthony confirmed as he followed Megan towards the small emergency department the hospital boasted. 'She's being brought in. She called me earlier, saying she didn't feel well and that she was going to go and lie down.'

'You here to meet the ambulance?' Loughlin asked as he sauntered towards her. She even liked the way he walked. Honestly, the man really was a well put-together package. He'd been rostered onto A and E duty that afternoon.

'My wife's *in* the ambulance,' Anthony explained. Megan's ordinarily calm and sedate registrar was now in a flap. Not that she blamed him. She liked Anthony's wife but if Romana was being brought in, if the paramedics were saying that she was in labour, it could mean an immediate transfer was needed to New South Wales Children's Hospital, where both mother and baby would be given better treatment.

'Ah. Right. Well, then. That puts a different spin on things.' Loughlin patted Anthony reassuringly on the shoulder.

'I'll get the transfer organised,' Megan said, and headed to the phone.

'Do you really think that's going to be necessary?' Anthony stared at his boss.

'It's Romana, Anthony. She's one of our own. I'm not taking any chances. Lochie and I are trained in emergency medicine as well as general surgery but not in prenatal obstetrics. This is one for the big boys.'

Loughlin couldn't keep the smile from his face as Megan

used his nickname. Again, it just went to illustrate that she was starting to thaw a little towards him, to let him peek through the cracks in the wall she'd built around herself. Most of the other staff had taken to calling him Lochie straight away but, as he'd already guessed, Megan wasn't the type of woman to let anyone into her inner sanctum and if she did, they'd need to earn the right.

He squared his shoulders, watching as she spoke firmly but calmly to Anthony. She really was brilliant. He'd known it yesterday when they'd been working together but after reading her articles…the woman had amazing insight and perception when it came to medicine and he appreciated her clever mind.

Anthony was still spluttering his protests. 'But work? The list?'

Megan placed a hand onto his shoulder. 'Irrelevant. From this point on you're officially on leave.' She nodded firmly and as she spoke into the telephone receiver, Lochie couldn't help but be impressed at the way she was taking charge of the situation.

She thought she was stand-offish, prickly, but she wasn't. She was doing her job. She didn't see herself as a member of this community but she was, especially as he'd just heard her use the phrase 'one of our own'. He wondered when *she* would realise that? Oh, yes, she was quite a woman.

By the time the ambulance arrived, the helicopter that would transfer the young family to Sydney was well on its way. Romana had received oxygen and salbutamol to try and stop labour.

'I'm hesitant to do an internal,' Megan said, 'in case I do more harm than good.' She checked the baby's heartbeat and was pleased with the effect the bronchodilator was having. 'There's no oedema of the feet or hands, which is a good sign.'

Nicole, who'd come off the ward to assist her friends, took Romana's blood pressure and attached the oximeter, which would measure the oxygen saturations at regular intervals. 'Blood pressure is elevated. Pulse is higher than normal but starting to steady.'

'Don't you have an ultrasound machine?' Loughlin asked, and

the look he gave Megan said that at that moment he was wishing for all of his big hospital equipment, which was usually right at his fingertips whenever he needed it.

'It's on its way.'

'Where is it? Did someone just take it out for a stroll?' His words made Romana smile and when she did, Anthony visibly relaxed. It was the right thing to say at the right moment and Megan was beginning to realise that Loughlin's gift of reading people, of understanding their emotions, was no doubt one of his biggest assets as far as his work went.

'We only have one sonographer on today and she's flat out.'

'*I'll* go and get it,' Loughlin volunteered. 'Just tell me where it is.'

'It's on its way,' Megan assured him. 'Now, Romana, I'd like you and Anthony to go to Sydney.'

'But things are settling,' Romana protested.

'Yes, they are, and whilst the baby's heartbeat is nice and strong, we want to keep it that way. Besides, this baby is special. You've had trouble in the past with keeping babies in this trimester. I'd prefer it if you had the best care possible for the rest of your pregnancy. Now, can you describe the sensations you had?' Megan wrote down what her patient told her and when the sonographer arrived with the ultrasound machine, they stepped aside to let the woman do her work.

'You all right?' Loughlin asked Megan, his words quiet.

'Sure. Why?'

'I don't know. You seem a wee bit…oh, I don't know how to say it…attached.'

'To whom?' Please, she prayed silently. Don't let him realise that I'm intrigued by him.

'By your patient and her husband.'

'Oh. Right. Well, Romana's a nice lady and Anthony's my colleague.'

Loughlin tut-tutted quietly and shook his head. 'They're your *friends*, Dr Megan Iris Edwards. You're nowhere near as friend-less as you think. And here I was, feeling sorry for you.'

'And I'm feeling sorry for you, too,' she teased quietly.

'Why is that?'

'Because you're going to be assisting me in Theatre all after-noon.'

'What about A and E?'

'Nicole can handle it and if not she can call you out, but that shouldn't happen. Not today.'

'Are you a psychic?'

She shook her head. 'Just a doctor who's learned the cycles of her hospital.'

'*Her* hospital? Not getting attached to the area, are you?'

'I am the clinical director, Lochie, so in essence, yes, it *is* my hospital and one I'm more than willing to hand over to the next clinical director before I leave. Ah…I think that's the chopper I hear.' She was glad of the diversion. With Loughlin standing so close to her, his breath fanning her cheek, the warmth from his body surrounding her own, the scent of his spicy cologne…it was all starting to distract her from her job. All of those things combined with his twinkling brown eyes made a rather lethal combination.

Megan checked the ultrasound screen, happy with the results, before heading out to the landing pad to meet the transfer staff. She'd needed to put some distance between herself and Loughlin McCloud. Not only was the man taking up much of her mental time, given that she couldn't help but think about him, he was also creating havoc with her body…and that was downright danger-ous as she had no idea how to control the way he made her feel.

It wasn't long before the little family was on board the chopper, Anthony looking more happy and relaxed about the whole situation. Romana had indeed stabilised but Megan wasn't taking any chances. She'd rather be safe than sorry, especially when she knew the couple had been trying to have a baby for quite some time. Besides, she'd become quite fond of her regis-trar and his pretty wife. Perhaps Loughlin was right. Perhaps she hadn't distanced herself as much as she'd initially thought.

'They're going to do just fine,' Loughlin said as he came up behind Megan, who was staring up into the sky as the helicop-ter took off, heading towards Sydney.

'I know. Romana's a strong woman. She'll make sure that her baby is all right.'

'True, but I meant the three of them together. As a family.'

'How can you tell?' Megan looked up at him and it was only then she realised how close they were to each other. The spicy scent she equated with Loughlin filled her senses and she took a small step backwards, hoping to put a bit of distance between them.

'Because I've been on the end of a bad marriage, a bad preg-nancy and a bad delivery.'

'Your daughter was premmie?'

'She was.' It had been the most dreadful, stressful time of Loughlin's life. Having Romana coming in had brought back memories, and where he thought he'd dealt with them all long ago, it surprised him to not only remember that time so vividly but to also feel a strong sense of Bonnie's betrayal.

The whole experience had been bitter-sweet. Heather's life had just begun and he'd been in awe of the baby who was his re-sponsibility. At the same time he'd also watched the mother of his child pull away from both of them as though she would become infected with something nasty if she stayed.

Megan noted the scowl on Loughlin's face and wondered what on earth he was thinking about to make his otherwise jovial features go so dark. She shivered a little and realised she never wanted him to look at her in such a way. Almost desperate to bring the smile back to his face, she placed a hand on his arm and grinned up at him. 'And I'll bet that Heather is now a strong and healthy preteen.'

It worked. His eyebrows lifted and so did his lips, but when he looked down at her, she could still see a hint of pain receding back into his memories. Megan couldn't believe how wonderful she felt at being able to lift his mood. It was delightful to see him smiling again.

'Strong, and stubborn, too.'

'Like her dad?'

'Aye.' His smile broadened.

'You miss her.' It was a statement, not a question.

'Och, aye, Megsy. She may be a hot-headed lassie but she's *my* hot-headed lassie. I feel as though half of me is missing when she's not around.'

'Where is she now? I mean, I know she's in Scotland but with whom?'

'With my sister.'

'And has she also inherited the bossy gene from her aunts?'

'Aye, she has. In spades!' Loughlin's nod was definite.

'That's good, then.'

'Why?'

'Because at least here in Australia you'll have someone to keep you in line.'

Loughlin fixed her with a determined stare. 'You wouldn't by any chance be teasing me again, would you, Dr Edwards?'

'Och, aye,' she responded, and was rewarded with a chuckle from her colleague.

It was great to see that twinkling light, that teasing glint back in Loughlin's eyes and Megan had to stop herself from sighing with pleasure. She'd managed to pull him from his bad memories and now she'd made him laugh. It made her feel good. Loughlin put his arm about Megan and gave her a little squeeze before quickly stepping back as though even that small touch had been too much. Megan's body buzzed alive with heated awareness.

'Come on.' His voice held a hint of huskiness and Megan wondered if he wasn't as immune to her as she'd initially thought.

'We have an operating list to get going with otherwise we won't make it to the shops on time before they shut.'

Even with the added patient to the list, Megan was a little sceptical whether they'd get through it *and* have time to shop, but she didn't say anything to Loughlin in case he thought she was being too pessimistic. Calvin had told her on countless occasions that she always looked at the glass as though it was half-empty, that she was slightly paranoid and highly possessive. In fact, Calvin had said so many things to her and each time she'd taken them as a criticism, working hard at the faults he'd pinpointed so that she would feel worthy of him.

As she stood at the scrub sink, she shook her head, unable to believe she'd let him do that to her. Her time here in Kiama had been enough for her to see how much of her life she'd lived for Calvin. Since then she'd been trying to figure out exactly who Megan Edwards was. She wasn't quite sure when she'd started to lose who she really was deep down inside but now she was determined to get the real Megan back. The only problem was, she wasn't really sure who that was any more and often found herself floundering in a sea of confusion.

She tried to breathe in deeply, the pains in her chest making themselves known. Closing her eyes, she tried to go through her relaxation exercises, hoping the pains would soon settle.

'You all right?' Loughlin's smooth voice washed over her and she looked up at him. 'You had a scowl on your forehead that would make even the scariest of monsters scamper away and hide.'

'I was thinking about my ex.'

'Ah. Well, that'll do it every time.' He began scrubbing his hands on the opposite side of the sink. 'My own scowl almost reaches my knees when I think about my ex.' He paused for a moment. 'Is that your ex-husband or ex-boyfriend or ex-something else?'

Megan wasn't sure whether to tell Loughlin or not. After all, she was desperately trying to keep her distance from him, to make sure their lives only intersected when it was absolutely necessary. However, he *had* opened up to her, telling her about his own ex. The pains in her chest tightened for a moment.

Loughlin leaned in a little closer, his scent teasing her nostrils, the heat from his body encompassing her. 'You don't have to tell me if you don't want to.' His voice was almost a whisper and, combined with the accent, Megan felt those pains in her chest start to ease a little. She knew it wasn't just his voice that had the relaxing effect on her but his whole presence.

When she'd first met him, by the side of the road with her car, she'd noticed a carefree attitude about him and had envied him that. Now, though, the more time she seemed to spend around him, the more she was starting to wonder whether he couldn't teach her a thing or two about how to relax…purely in a platonic friendly-colleagues sort of way, of course.

She looked into his eyes and gave a little shrug. 'Ex-fiancé.'

'Ooh. That doesn't sound good.'

'No, especially as he became my ex when he left me at the altar.'

Loughlin's expression instantly softened to one of understanding and concern. 'Oh, Megsy.' He placed a caring hand on her shoulder. It explained a lot about her. About why she was so brittle, so prickly, so distant. It hadn't escaped his notice that she tried to keep a barrier between herself and her colleagues and now he knew why. 'You don't want to get close to anyone again because it means you can take control of your life and avoid being hurt in the same way.'

'Exactly. I know I'm not the first woman to be left at the altar and I probably won't be the last.'

'And it's the reason you needed to get away, to come to Kiama.' He nodded as more puzzle pieces seemed to fit into place.

'Yes. I want to know what freedom is.' Megan shook her head. 'It's hard to explain but I've always done the right thing. All my life. School was easy, I advanced rapidly, I loved medicine. My future seemed bright, laid out before me in a clear and concise path. And then…I met Calvin.' Megan shook her head, looking away from Loughlin. 'He…I never realised how controlling he was until it was too late. I never realised how badly he'd damaged my confidence until I moved here.' Megan dragged in a deep breath and pulled herself back under control, fighting away the tears she'd thought she'd finished shedding a long time ago. Although this time they felt as though they were tears of frustration…frustration at her previous ignorance, rather than tears of pain and heartbreak.

'I just wish I wasn't the sort of person to play and replay everything over and over in my head, trying to figure out where it was that I went wrong.'

Loughlin nodded as though he knew exactly what she was talking about. 'You'll drive yourself around the twist with that sort of thinking. What you need to do is every time one of those terrible memories lodges itself in your brain, you access a different, more pleasant memory—preferably with bigger boots— to kick the stinking one out.'

'Easier said than done.'

'Nay, it's true. I'm the same as you. I have a constant replay of Bonnie standing there in her designer clothes, telling me she doesn't want to have the baby. That she wants to book herself in for an abortion.'

Megan's eyes widened at his words. She looked around the room in case there was anyone else about but at the moment it was just the two of them at the scrub sink and he'd dropped his voice so that only she could hear his words.

'Oh, Loughlin. No.' Her shock must have shown on her face because he nodded.

'Och, aye. My wife was willing to terminate my daughter's life rather than have a ruined figure. She was selfish, she was a lying, cheating, backstabbing woman, and I hadn't seen it until that very moment.'

'And that's the memory which you have stuck on constant replay?'

He nodded, his expression solemn. 'Used to be. Every time something went wrong in my life, that's the one which would go straight to number one…with a bullet.'

'So how did you stop it?'

'I replaced it with a better memory. A stronger memory.'

'Which one?'

'The one where I held Heather in my arms for the very first time.' The smile on his lips was big and bright and natural, oozing with fatherly pride. There could be no doubt about how much this man loved his daughter.

'That must have been an incredible time for you.'

'The best.' He stared off into the distance for a moment, a look of sheer adoration on his face as he remembered the instant he'd held his daughter in his arms. 'She was so tiny. So helpless. And then she curled her wee fingers around my pinkie and stole my heart.' His voice was soft, gentle and filled with absolute love. Then his eyes flicked to meet hers. 'And so, Megan Iris Edwards, what we need to do for you is to find a memory that is strong enough to wipe anything else from your mind.'

'I wouldn't have a clue where to begin. I had a happy childhood. Perhaps I could pick one from there.' She elbowed off the taps and reached for a sterile drape.

'It needs to be stronger than something from your childhood. It needs to be forceful and passionate. Something with real…power.' His gaze settled on her lips for a split second and Megan's heart rate instantly increased. What on earth could he mean?

'We'll work on it later, Dr Edwards.' He winked at her as a nurse came in to help them gown and glove. The smile he'd given her, combined with his wink, had made her feel as though she was someone special and she found it was actually enough to help her focus her mind on the list ahead, rather than the failures of her past.

Their first patient was in for removal of a hernia and after Megan had opened, she discovered the hernia was strangulated.

'Game on,' she announced as she looked at it.

'A fitting beginning for our first theatre session together.' Loughlin looked at her over the patient and she could tell, even though he was wearing a mask, that he was smiling.

'All right, Dr McCloud. Let's see just how good you are. Take the lead.'

'As you said, Dr Edwards—game on.' They shifted positions so that she was assisting him and she had to admit he had deft skill when it came to excising strangulated hernias. 'So how did I do?' he asked once they'd finished. They had a quick break whilst the theatre was cleaned and Megan leaned back against the cupboard and looked him over, nodding as she allowed her gaze to travel over him from head to toe and back again.

'Not bad.'

'What? Are you talking about me as a man because if you want to give me a few more looks like that, feel free, Megsy.' There it was again, his natural flirting charm that had her all in a dither.

Embarrassment started to rise within her as she realised exactly what she'd done, quite unconsciously…or perhaps it was that her subconscious was taking control and making her behave like the woman she *wanted* to be. Not that she wanted to go around ogling her colleagues but if she was actually attracted to someone that she might…just might…be able to let go and see where the moment took her.

Self-confidence. That's what it all came down to and right now Loughlin was actually inviting her to look once more. She wanted to. There was no doubt about that. So why shouldn't she? This is what her move to Kiama was supposed to be about. Letting go. Doing different things, and *this* was most definitely different. Megan pushed away the embarrassment she was fighting and decided to take him up on his offer, her eyes sliding again over his magnificent body.

He was tall. She liked that about him. He was trim, too, and although the scrubs hung loosely on his lithe frame, she could quite easily see he had well-formed biceps and strong, lean shoulders. Finally, she met his eyes. Their gazes locked and held. Megan was a little surprised to find his seemed to be filled with equal appreciation and it was only then she realised that while she'd been looking closely at him, he'd been looking closely at her.

Her throat went instantly dry and she felt a blush tinge her cheeks, although this time it wasn't from embarrassment but more from the knowledge that he'd obviously liked what he'd seen. She knew she wasn't beautiful but when Loughlin looked at her like that, she could almost believe that she was.

'You… Ah…' She couldn't believe how breathless her words were sounding. Clearing her throat, she tried again but found herself powerless to look away. 'You did good, Lochie.'

'I like it when you call me that.' Her Australian accent combined with the present huskiness in her tone made his name sound rich and sexy. Although he may have had little romantic involvement in the past, no one had ever made his name sound so sexy before.

'Really?' Why did that fill her with another wave of excitement? Their words were quiet and intimate and even though they were almost on different sides of the scrub room, it was as though they were alone in the universe with no need to shout.

'Megan. Can you take a look at this?' Theatre Sister came into the room, her attention on a piece of paper she was holding, but it was enough to break the moment and Megan was quick to look away. She returned her attention to the work at hand but had difficulty concentrating due to her awareness of Loughlin. Even as he moved around the room, she could sense exactly where he was even if she couldn't see him.

Their list continued, as did her impressions of her new colleague. He certainly was well qualified and she was pleased the hospital had snapped him up. Not only would he help to lighten her own workload until her contract expired but where the patients and this community were concerned, she knew she could trust him. He would no doubt slip into the role of director once she left and it was a fact that he'd make a darned fine head of the hospital. She could trust him with that, too.

The big question was, though, was he someone she could trust in other areas of her life?

CHAPTER SIX

'I THINK this one.'

'I disagree. I think she'd like this one.' Loughlin bounced on a white single bed which had pretty white flowers painted around the foot- and headboards.

'Sure. If she was five.'

He stuck his tongue out at Megan. 'Well, what would you know about it?'

Megan laughed. 'Uh…perhaps the fact that I'm a girl might help. Look, don't get your sporran in a twist. Come and take another look at this one.'

'It's a double bed!'

'Exactly. Every girl coming into their teenage years would give their last lot of baby teeth for a double bed.' She put a hand on the mattress and pressed down a few times.

'But it…it's just so…big. She'd be so small in it.'

'She'd feel like she was growing up and that you were taking her seriously.'

'I do take her seriously.'

'I'm sure you do. I'm sure you're the best daddy in the world.'

'Too right, mate.' He attempted an Australian accent as he spoke and Megan simply shook her head, a smile tugging at her lips. He really was a lot of fun to be around. She hadn't realised picking out a bed for a girl she hadn't even met would be so entertaining.

'No. Don't do that. Stick to Scottish. Leave the tough accents to those of us who can do them properly.'

'Hey. It wasn't that bad,' he said defensively, and she shook her head again.

'Come over here and take a closer look at this bed.' Megan beckoned him over and tried to hide her smile as he reluctantly walked towards her, his shoulders slumped in defeat, his knuckles almost dragging on the floor. She smothered a giggle.

'Try it out. It's a comfortable mattress. It's not too big and it will definitely fit into the bedroom.'

'How would you know? You've never been to my house.'

'It's the same as mine or hadn't you realised that?'

He broke from his bad acting and smiled at her. 'Of course I did. Just didn't realise you knew that.' He lay back, bouncing around again as though trying to get comfortable. 'I don't know. There's heaps of room. Lie down and test it out.'

Megan's eyes widened at the thought of lying down next to him. 'Uh…it's fine. I think you can test this out by yourself.'

'Nay. Lie down and try it out. You're the one who's insisting I buy it.' There was a hint of indignation in his tone.

'I'm the one who's insisting you lower your voice.'

'If you don't lie down next to me, I'll not only *not* lower my voice but I won't buy it either. A lose-lose situation.' He watched indecision flit across her face as she quickly looked around the store, trying to gauge which option she should take. 'What's it going to be, Megsy?'

Megan looked at him, lying there on that big bed. He looked so good. So bright and cheerful and welcoming. No. She couldn't possibly lie down next to him. She feigned nonchalance and shrugged her shoulders. 'So, fine. Don't buy it.'

'But I value your opinion. How can you give me an opinion if you don't lie down on it?'

He valued her opinion? Megan stared at him and was astonished to find tears starting to well in her eyes.

'Megan?' He stopped springing around on the mattress and lifted himself up so he was leaning on his side, head propped up on his elbow. His hair had spiked even further from all his shifting about and there was a definite twinkle in his eyes. 'What's the matter?'

'Nothing.' She looked away. He was far too appealing and she couldn't believe how his words had made her feel. She brushed a hand across her eyes, wiping away the small teardrops, and then sniffed. 'You'd best buy it, Loughlin, or else you'll need to go to Sydney to choose a bed for her. This is the only bedding shop in the Gerringong-Kiama district.'

'OK, then.'

When she felt his hand on her shoulder she jumped, not realising he'd moved. 'Megsy. What's wrong?'

'It's nothing. I'm just being silly.'

'Never. How about we go for coffee? Your treat.'

That made her smile a little. 'Gee, thanks.'

'Hey, it's cheaper than another dinner date.'

'True. Do you want to get the bed sorted out?'

'It can wait until tomorrow.' And then he surprised her further by taking her hand in his and leading her from the store, telling the salesman that he'd be back to buy the double bed tomorrow and to have it ready.

Hand in hand, they crossed the road to a small coffee-shop, which was deserted, the owners getting ready to close up for the night. Megan was about to suggest that they just head home when she realised Loughlin had sweet-talked the owner into not only staying open but to make them a fresh pot of French pressed coffee.

'A talk like this demands good coffee,' he stated as they sat down. He'd let go of her hand and she was now able to start settling the excessive beating of her heart. His touch had been sweet, innocent and yet she hadn't been able to control the effect this man had on her. Problem was, it was only getting stronger and a lot harder to fight.

She knew he was a charmer. It was quite evident when all the female staff at the hospital seemed to almost swoon whenever he walked into the room. It was another reason why she should avoid any sort of personal contact with him…such as sitting alone with him in a coffee-shop in the evening.

'So…' he said after a brief pause. 'Why the tears?'

Megan shook her head, feeling highly self-conscious. She realised he wasn't going to let her off the hook and decided it would be easier to rip the sticking plaster off in one quick go rather than prolong the agony. 'Why the tears? Simply because you wanted my opinion. See? I told you it was nothing.'

'Why wouldn't I want your opinion? You're a smart woman.' He watched her closely and then realisation began to dawn. 'You haven't been asked for your opinion much before?'

'Not on anything non-medical. Not by Calvin—he's my ex, by the way. It's not a nice feeling to be in a relationship and one day realise that you don't matter.' She tried to speak the words in a matter-of-fact way without her voice breaking. She almost succeeded.

'He didn't appreciate you.' His words were a statement and not for the first time Megan was struck with the sense that Loughlin knew exactly how she was feeling. He could only do that if he'd been in a similar place with his own ex-wife.

'No. The problem was I started to realise that even *I* didn't trust my opinions. I didn't have the confidence.'

'He'd stripped it all away.'

'Yes, and I have no clue when that happened.'

'Had you known him a long time before wanting to marry him?'

'Yes. We'd been dating for a long time. We met at work when he was a registrar. Calvin was older than me and so when he became a consultant, things changed.'

'Personally as well as medically?'

'Yes. I knew he'd be busier, that he'd have more pressure. He's currently Head of Cardiology at Sydney's leading cardiac hospital, and he's only in his early forties.'

'A surgeon who thinks he's God. Well, most cardiologists do. And neurosurgeons, for that matter.' Loughlin leaned back in his chair as their coffee was delivered to their table. 'They look down on us other surgeons as not being able to cut the grade. At least, that's the way it was back home.'

Megan's smile was tired as she sipped her coffee. 'Things aren't so different on this side of the world.'

'So why get married?'

'Because I asked him. It was a leap year, on February 29, and, as you know, it's traditional for the woman to ask the man on that day. I sort of entered into it in a joking fashion…'

'Protecting yourself just in case he said no.'

'Yes, but I've at least admitted to myself that I took the opportunity to ask him because I thought he'd never get around to asking me.'

'I take it he agreed.'

'He did. He said it made perfect sense, that it was the next step in our relationship. And then he told me to organise the wedding and let him know where and when to turn up.'

'He didn't receive the memo?'

Megan sighed, amazed to find that for the first time since her disastrous aborted wedding day she didn't have that overwhelming tightness in her chest when she talked about it. 'Apparently not. He did, however, send a message through his registrar to let me know he was not only stuck in Theatre but that he'd be stuck there for quite some time. Such as for ever. He called me later that night to tell me he'd rethought the decision and decided it would be best if we dissolved our partnership rather than move forward.'

'Those were the words he used?'

'Almost verbatim.'

Loughlin shook his head. 'And, let me guess, the time you spent with him diminished your confidence in yourself, made you doubt and second-guess your decisions and in the end you had no idea who you were?'

He seemed to be looking into her soul. Megan watched him closely and she saw that the main reason he'd been able to read her was because he knew what she'd been through. First hand. 'Been there?'

'Done that. Look, let's not worry about our pasts. That's what we need to put behind us. To move on. To get revenge by being deliriously happy without them.' He poured the coffee. 'Now that you've shared so much of your past with me, there's one burning question I need to ask you.'

Megan's eyed widened at that. What could he want to know? What was he about to say?

'Megan Iris, there comes a time in all new relationships— whether they're friendships or something more—when that all-too-important question needs to be asked.'

Megan's eyes were intent on his, wondering what on earth he was going to ask her. She held her breath, waiting with anticipation. Loughlin held out the sugar bowl to her.

'One lump or two?'

It took a second for his words to register. 'That's the important question?'

'That's it for tonight. One lump or two?'

She smiled and shook her head, delighted with the way he could continue to tease when she was in the middle of deep emotional discoveries. Well, they had been taught that laughter was the best medicine and it appeared that Loughlin was a confirmed practitioner of it.

As they drove home from their shopping expedition, Loughlin's thoughts were on the woman beside him, trying to figure out just when he'd become so interested in her. For all intents and purposes he hardly knew Megan Iris Edwards, but by the same token they seemed to share some sort of connection, as though they *had* known each other for quite some time. The only other woman he'd been this relaxed around in the past had been

Bonnie. That in itself should be enough impetus to make him run for the hills. Yet he wasn't.

What was wrong with him? Although he'd dated in the past, he'd managed to keep everything under control until it had become absolutely necessary for him to break things off. He guarded his heart carefully, determined it would never get broken or ripped into little pieces ever again. Heather was his number-one priority and he'd always used her as an excuse.

Perhaps that was why he was even contemplating stepping into territory he usually avoided. Heather wasn't here and for the first time since her birth he was on his own. Albeit it was only for two more weeks, but it made him realise just how much of his life he'd lived for Heather and his sisters. Not having any of them around now gave him a clear illustration of how lonely his life was without them. One day Heather would be grown and striking out on a life of her own. Then where would he be? An old man, sitting alone at home of an evening with a rug on his knees, watching telly? Not a chance.

Megan wasn't Bonnie. That was something else he had to keep remembering. When they'd initially met, he'd thought she was a career-woman and he guessed she still was, but she was not the ambitious, money motivated type his ex-wife had been. Instead, she was a well-organised hospital director with a caring attitude, an amazing mind and a loving bedside manner—even if she didn't admit to the last. The patients thought the world of her, that much was true, and he'd already heard the gossip that she probably wouldn't renew her contract when the time came, even though everyone wanted her to.

The community had embraced her, helped her to heal, and he'd also witnessed Megan giving back just as much to the people she cared for. Whilst she thought she was holding herself aloof from her colleagues, she was already one of them. She simply hadn't realised it yet.

He glanced across at her. She wasn't classically beautiful but, then, classically beautiful women weren't his type at all. He liked them a little flawed, a little obsessive and a little neurotic. He smiled to himself. Megan was fitting that bill quite nicely. He thought back to the moment they'd shared earlier in the scrub room. He'd had an overwhelming urge to kiss her. To make a memory that would wipe all the bad memories away. Thankfully they'd been interrupted or he might have ended up making a grave mistake.

Or would he?

What would it be like to kiss the complex woman sitting beside him? The urge hadn't disappeared, as he'd expected it to. Was she like Bonnie? Would the risk of attempting an involvement with Megan end in heartbreak? She had plans to leave Kiama. She'd been badly hurt in the past. So what did the present hold?

Megan shifted in her seat and Loughlin made sure his attention was on the road before them. He could feel her looking at him for a moment before she spoke, her tone as smooth as silk and washing over him as such.

'Thanks for tonight, Lochie. It was nice to go out and just do something completely different for a change.'

'Let me guess—you usually go home from the hospital with a briefcase filled with work and spend the night catching up on everything else you didn't have time to complete during the day.'

'Yes. Sad, isn't it?'

'No.' The one word was spoken with earnestness. 'Not sad, Megsy. Just a way of coping until something better comes along. And for the record, I enjoyed myself too—although you still should have tried out that bed.'

'Let's not go there again.' Even now the thought of lying next to him on that bed made her body warm with delight. The man beside her was starting to affect her far more than she liked. Today had been another case in point where she appeared to be completely conscious of where he was at all times. His presence was overwhelming her and she wasn't sure how to deal with that.

To that end, she knew she needed to put a bit of distance between them…somehow.

Loughlin turned the corner and drove up the track that would soon lead them to her door. She needed to say something now, to get the words out sooner rather than later. Clearing her throat, she looked at him. 'There's also something I need to tell you.'

'What's that?'

'Well…I've really appreciated the lift to and from work today but I won't need you to pick me up tomorrow.'

He glanced over at her, his eyebrows hitting his hairline. 'Got your car fixed, then?'

'Not exactly. I had it towed to a garage this morning and also arranged for a hire car to be delivered to my home. It should be there by now. I've also asked Jasper to try and find me a new car to buy. There's a lot more choice in Sydney.'

Loughlin processed this information. Part of him was a little disappointed because he'd quite enjoyed being a knight in shining armour and helping out. He liked helping people. It gave him a buzz, but whilst he'd enjoyed spending a bit more time with Megan, especially away from the hospital atmosphere, he also knew she was right to put more distance between them. 'Fair enough.'

'Don't think I don't appreciate your gesture to drive me to and from the hospital until my car problem is solved. It's just that it wouldn't always be practical. We'll be leaving the hospital at different times and then there are house calls to take into consideration and other things I need to do, like—'

'It's OK, Megsy. You don't need to explain. I completely understand. Of course you need your freedom and independence. I'm just glad I could help out in your wee emergency.'

'Well, as I said, I've really appreciated it.'

He pulled up outside her home and turned the engine off. For a split second Megan wondered if he was planning to walk her to the door…or come inside? Did he want another cup of coffee? If he did, he'd have to have it black because she hadn't had any time to buy groceries today, even though he'd declared last night that they would. Unsure what was going to happen next, Megan undid her seat belt and turned slightly to face him, her heartbeat increasing in the sudden silence that surrounded them.

'Well…thanks for the lift home.' She put her hand on the door lever but Loughlin stopped her.

'Wait a second. I know we didn't get around to buying groceries for you tonight but there's also something else we've forgotten to do.'

'Oh?' Her gaze flicked from his eyes to his lips and back again as he spoke. The automatic sensor light had switched on when he'd driven up but even in the shadows she could see he was looking intently at her.

'We haven't made your replacement memory.'

Megan swallowed, unsure exactly what he meant. 'Sorry?' She watched as he undid his own seat belt and leaned closer towards her.

The atmosphere in the car escalated to overpowering and her heart pounded as her mouth went dry. Her lips parted to allow the pent-up air to escape as she looked into his eyes.

'We need to make a nice memory for you so that you can replay it when the bad ones intrude.'

Excited anticipation started to rise within her as she wondered exactly what he had in mind. He wanted to make a nice memory and he was looking at her as though she was the most stunning woman in the world! The pounding of her heart accelerated from feverish to intoxicated. 'I…uh…think I'll be…uh…fine.' Her words were stilted and she tried to swallow, tried to ignore the way his nearness was making her feel.

He raised an eyebrow at her words, a gleam of desire entering his dark eyes. 'I think you will, too.' With that, he didn't give her time to say another word as he pressed his mouth to hers.

Megan gasped at the contact, surprised and totally unsure what to do for that first split second. Lochie's lips were on hers. They were warm, soft and nice…*very* nice. Slowly they moved over her own as though he didn't want to rush her, didn't want this memory he was insistent on making to be a hot and powerful one.

Seduction. That was the word that came instantly to mind as her head continued to whirl with excitement. He wasn't forcing her into doing anything and she knew if she hadn't wanted him to kiss her, she could have pulled away by now. But she hadn't and that thought alone caused her stomach to churn with nervous butterflies.

She sighed and relaxed a smidgen and Loughlin took that as a sign of acceptance. The way she'd spoken about her ex, the way the pain had come into her eyes, pierced her soul…he'd seen her hurt. She'd *allowed* him to see her hurt. Whether this kiss meant anything to her or whether it was just a means of helping her to move on with her life, to realise that she was a strong woman who didn't need to wrap herself in a prickly exterior to get by for the rest of her life, he had no idea.

All he knew was that when he'd set out to kiss her, he'd wanted to show her that the world of romance hadn't ended when she'd been left a jilted bride. He'd wanted to show her that he thought she was a good person. He'd wanted to show her that she could go on making happy memories, that her world hadn't stopped.

Of course, by the same token she could have wrenched back from his touch and slapped him across the face. Thank the sweet Lord above that that hadn't been her reaction. He was more than pleased that she'd accepted his strange therapy for making a new memory. What he hadn't bargained for was the way her response was starting to fuel his own.

He was kissing Megan. His new colleague. His new neighbour… And he was liking it far more than he'd anticipated. Her confidence was beginning to grow and she started to take the initiative, her tongue slipping out to part his lips.

A powerful surge of hunger burst through him as the real taste of her mouth entered his own and he found it delectably sweet and enticing. He'd planned to keep the kiss soft and light but now primal urges were starting to war within him and the desire to haul her into his arms, holding her chest firmly against his own, were becoming too pressing to ignore…but ignore them he did.

Gently. Slowly. Delicately. This woman's confidence had been destroyed and he wasn't going to do anything to jeopardise her getting it back, and moving too far, too fast would surely do that. Besides, the way her mouth was moving over his, the way she was taking charge of this kiss, was beginning to make him question himself.

She was absolutely delightful with the way her confidence seemed to increase with each passing second. Where she may have had doubts about her attractiveness after having her heart shattered so badly, *his* responsiveness was obviously helping her to realise she had much more to give. He wanted her to realise she was a highly desirable woman and that he, for one, found her immensely attractive.

He also couldn't believe how right she felt in his arms…especially when she was no doubt all wrong for him. Megan had her own problems, her own baggage, which was really nothing to do with him. He knew he couldn't solve the problems of the world but he could at least control his own. Megan needed a man who would take things slowly with her, who would help restore her trust and faith in men. Although he liked to help people, to be there to support them, this wasn't the type of intense and heart-stopping support he'd been planning on giving.

He'd been too burned by Bonnie. Not just once. Not even twice but three times. Three times his ex-wife had managed to rip his heart out and leave him a mere shell of a man. He had his own problems to deal with and whilst he was more than happy to be friends with Megan, to be friends with anyone who wanted friendship, he had to keep his priorities and need for self-preservation upper most in his mind.

At that thought, he placed his hands on Megan's shoulders,

allowing himself ten more glorious seconds of pleasure before he eased away. He watched as she slowly opened her eyes, eyes that were glazed with a mixture of longing and regret.

Neither of them spoke, silence reigning in the car. Megan looked at Loughlin's dark eyes, not exactly sure what she expected to see there but, given that the sensor light had now switched off, she couldn't see much at all. Her gaze flicked back to his lips, which were now pursed as though he was trying to stop himself from repeating what they'd just been doing.

His hands were still on her shoulders and the warmth that was emanating from them was sending small electrical waves through her body, keeping the jolts, the churning in her stomach simmering on low.

As if he realised belatedly he was still touching her, he lifted his hands and jerked them away, easing back to the other side of the car. 'Uh… Megan. I'm—'

'Sorry?' She cut him off. She knew instinctively that was what he'd been about to say and she didn't want to hear it. Her voice was low, calm and controlled. She made sure of that. She was a woman who'd stood at the front of a church before all of her family members and close friends. She was the one who'd told them all that Calvin had changed his mind, that he'd decided not to marry her—and she hadn't shed a tear. In truth, she couldn't have cried even if she'd tried because frankly she'd been too numb. Calvin hadn't wanted her.

Now, after a mind-numbing, sense-whirling, heart-pounding kiss, it appeared Loughlin wasn't all that interested in her either.

'It's fine, Loughlin. You don't need to apologise. I realise you were trying to be nice, thinking that perhaps that if you kissed me it might wipe out the memories I have of my fiancé kissing me, but it didn't work out. Silly plan, really. Not sure you'd thought all of the angles through.'

'You've got that straight,' he muttered softly, raking an unsteady hand through his hair. He'd only meant to give her a light, friendly kiss. To let her know that she was an attractive woman… But then she'd opened her mouth and allowed him to experience the real essence of her. He'd been captivated by her. Repressed emotions he hadn't wanted to think about in many years had surged their way to the forefront, demanding he pay them attention. Kissing Megan Edwards had given him more than he'd bargained for and right now, as he watched her lips move, he couldn't think of anything else except holding her in his arms again and repeating the action over and over.

And that would be wrong.

'It was a beezer of a mistake.'

'A *what* of a mistake?' Megan could feel the tightness in her chest returning as her anxiety levels rose, even though Loughlin's accent was getting stronger as he became more agitated.

'Er…huge. It means huge. Look, Megan. I didn't mean it. The kiss, I mean. We shouldn't have. *I* shouldn't have. I just didn't expect you to…' He trailed off, shaking his head. He may not be able to see the exact look on her face due to the darkness of the car but he could sense her attitude towards him, and it wasn't a friendly one. Rightly so. He needed to push her away, to put some distance between them, but by the same token he didn't want her to think that the kiss hadn't meant anything—because it had.

'It's only a mistake because I…and then you…and I…I hadn't expected and…' He stopped and took a deep breath. 'I was out of line. I'm sorry. I had no right taking advantage of you like that. Of your vulnerability when you were feeling so bad about your past, and—'

'Stop! Just stop.' Megan shook her head and held up one hand. 'I don't want to hear your excuses. I don't want to discuss it further. Not now. Not ever. We're colleagues and that's it.' She would forget about him, about how he'd just kissed her in the most exquisite, glorious way she'd ever experienced. And she'd remember how he'd admitted it was a *beezer* of a mistake.

Her hand fumbled for the door-handle. She needed to get out

of his car, get out of this confined space and into her own private sanctuary before she broke down in tears. Once again, she was being rejected. 'I'll also thank you not to try and make any other memories for me, Loughlin McCloud. No doubt this humiliating one can be added to the pile I already hold so dear to my heart.' Her voice broke at the end of her words and tears welled in her eyes. She turned towards the door, which was refusing to open, and stared blurry-eyed at the stupid lever, which was refusing to let her out.

He quickly climbed out and came around to the passenger side, opening the door for her.

'Thank you,' she all but spat at him as she walked blindly past him towards her house.

'Wait.' He was after her in a second. The sensor light had come back on, momentarily blinding both of them. 'Megsy. Wait.'

'Don't call me that,' she said, furious with herself for allowing him to get under her skin. He was her colleague. He'd kissed her. It had been nice but it had also been a mistake. She would get over this. She'd recovered from worse. She fumbled in her bag for her house keys.

'Megan. I'm sorry.'

'So you've said.' She'd found her keys and was trying to fit the key into the door but was disgusted to find her hand was trembling so much the simple action was becoming an impossibility. 'Now go away and leave me alone.'

He didn't move and she could feel him watching her. What more did he want? Hadn't he humiliated her enough for one night? Tears started to gather in her eyes, blurring her vision and making it even more impossible to get the stupid key in the stupid door.

In the next instant Loughlin took it from her, infuriating her even more by sliding it neatly into the lock and opening her door.

'Thank you.' The words were spoken between clenched teeth as she went inside, desperately needing to be in her own comfort zone before she completely lost control over her emotions. As she turned her back to him, she swiped at both her eyes, getting rid of the tears which were obscuring her vision.

'You're very polite when you're angry.'

'Stop being cute. Stop trying to get me out of a bad mood with your charm and charisma. Go and use it on the other females in this town. Go and make memories with the other women. Go and do whatever it is you want to do but just don't do it with me.' Her voice was filled with pain although she was desperately trying to squash it, to remain as much in control as she possibly could whilst he still stood before her.

It hadn't been this difficult for her to announce that her wedding had been called off. It hadn't been this difficult when she'd first seen Calvin after the aborted wedding—flirting outrageously with three of the cardiac nurses and totally ignoring her. Why? Why was standing here feeling humiliated before Loughlin McCloud so difficult to deal with?

He opened his mouth to say something but she turned away. 'Just go. Leave this prickly little echidna alone in her prickly little house, in her prickly little world.'

When he didn't move, when she caught a glimpse of the concern on his face, she did the only thing left for her to do. She shut the door and turned off the outside light.

The darkness of the night engulfed her, and she welcomed it.

CHAPTER SEVEN

FOR the next few days, Megan was determined to show Loughlin that he meant nothing to her. She was controlling her anxiety levels with deep-breathing exercises and rewarding herself with bubble baths in the evening after completing her paperwork. She needed to control her thoughts just as much and every day told herself for the next month or so until her contract expired. Then she could move on. With that in mind, she started to search for jobs, toying with the idea of going overseas for a while to really get away from everything.

Loughlin's attitude towards her was polite and mildly friendly, as though he was definitely watching himself around his prickly echidna boss. He didn't flirt with her, which must have been difficult because it seemed to be second nature for him, and kept all necessary contact between them clear and concise.

Yesterday, just over a week since he'd kissed her, that had changed. He'd come into her office after clinic and perched himself on the edge of her desk.

'How are things going, Megsy?'

She hadn't looked up, intent on showing him how busy she was by gathering up her papers and putting them into her briefcase. She'd ignored the way his spicy scent had wound its way about her along with the way his smooth tones made her legs turn to jelly. She'd stayed sitting down.

'Fine, thank you, Loughlin.' There was no point in telling him not to call her Megsy because it would only highlight the intimacy they'd previously shared. When he didn't say anything more, Megan wondered how much longer he'd stay. Didn't he get the hint that she didn't want to see him? To talk to him? Unless he had a query about hospital protocol or a patient, she wanted him out of her office.

He waited. Not saying a word but watching the way she was focused on packing her bag, getting ready to leave for the night. He checked his watch. It was almost six o'clock, early for Megan to leave—and he was pleased with that. She would usually stay a lot later and he'd been concerned about the way she was throwing herself completely into her work. However, he'd also realised that that was how she coped with the ups and downs in her life. It was the 'work would see her through' mentality. He'd used it before as well and discovered it wasn't good for his general health or stress levels.

Now, though, he would sit here and wait for her to give him her attention. To stop fussing about and actually look at him.

'Was there something in particular you wanted?' The words were crisp, clear, and yet there was a touch of impatience in her tone. She still didn't look at him.

'Not really. Just wanted to know how you were.'

'I've already answered that question. Now, if you'll excuse me…' Megan picked up the last lot of papers from her desk, annoyed to find her hand slightly trembling due to Loughlin's nearness. She went to put them in her briefcase but in her haste to get out of the confines of her office—and therefore out of Loughlin's presence—as quickly as possible, she accidentally knocked her bag to the floor, papers scattering all over the place.

Impatience and frustration rose to the fore and, gritting her teeth, she slid from her chair to gather them all up, not caring what order they were in. Loughlin, being the helpful man that he was, came around her desk and bent to assist her.

She had almost all the papers back in the bag, being careful not to touch his hands when he handed her the rest. 'Thank you.'

'You're welcome.' They were both still crouched on the floor. 'Megsy. Look at me.'

'No.'

'Please?'

Annoyance rising in her chest, she lifted her chin, allowing their gazes to meet. 'What do you want, Loughlin?'

'I want us to be friends.'

'We're colleagues. That's just going to have to do.' She rose and closed her briefcase, thankful that her legs seemed to be behaving themselves and could actually support her.

He stood up, the heat from his body close enough to envelop her. She ignored the sensation. 'It was just a kiss.'

'If you say so.' She walked away from him, heading towards the door.

'I didn't mean to hurt you. I'm sorry.'

Megan stopped for a moment but didn't turn around. Loughlin watched her closely, not liking the bad blood that currently existed between them. Would she turn? Say she forgave him? Say that she wanted to start again? Just be friends? They'd both been hurt so badly in the past that neither of them were willing to take that step forward but surely friendship wasn't out of the question?

'Please lock the door on your way out,' was all she said, before leaving him standing in her office, staring after her.

A week later, Megan was sitting in the tearoom, enjoying a quiet cuppa after a busy surgical list, when both Anthony and Nicole came into the room. It didn't take a rocket scientist to guess who they were talking about.

'To say he's settled into life in this small seaside village is an understatement,' Nicole was saying. 'It's as though he's always lived here, that he's always been around, that he's always been supporting our little community.'

'He just…fits,' Anthony agreed as they sat down.

'He does.' Nicole nodded enthusiastically. Megan wanted to walk out but knew it might look suspicious. 'Add to that the fact that he's not at all difficult to look at and it becomes a pleasure coming to work every day.' She sighed with longing as though she was remembering just how good-looking Loughlin was. 'It's about time we had some talent around here for us single girls to look at. Right, Megan?'

'If you say so, Nicole.'

'Are you feeling all right?' Anthony's tone was tinged with concern. 'You haven't been yourself for a while.'

'Busy.'

'Oh, are you writing more articles?' Nicole wanted to know. 'I read your last one. As usual, it was very good. You'll educate the masses of up-and-coming surgeons out there yet.'

'As well as the ones who are already qualified,' Anthony added with a smile. 'You have a talent for explaining even the most complex of equations to those of us whose minds don't work as quickly as yours.'

'Thank you.' Megan wasn't writing articles, though, in fact, she was supposed to be getting ready to submit to the journal again, but her thoughts had most definitely been elsewhere and that wasn't like her at all. Work was what she lived for now. Not handsome Scotsmen who went about kissing people and then declaring it to be a mistake.

She kept glancing at the door just in case Loughlin walked in, especially to find Nicole declaring to all and sundry how handsome she thought he was. Loughlin, not that she was keeping tabs on him, had been rushing around that morning like a chicken with its head cut off, but for the last few hours she hadn't seen him anywhere. She presumed he'd headed out to do some emergency house calls but she also wasn't about to ask anyone. The last thing she wanted was to draw attention to the fact that she was interested in Loughlin's every move. Because she wasn't.

LUCY CLARK   103

'So…Anthony. Tell me about Romana. How is she coping?' Megan had been glad when Romana had been admitted to the New South Wales Children's Hospital where she was still being closely monitored.

'She's doing OK. It's not easy being apart but I keep telling her it's only for a little while. The baby will be born soon enough and we both want her to be as healthy as possible.'

Megan smiled. 'Glad it's a girl?'

'Most definitely, although with the way Lochie's been in a tizz about his own daughter coming, I'm beginning to wonder.'

Anthony spoke the truth. Loughlin had been busy buying more basic furniture so Heather would be at least comfortable when she arrived. He'd also bought basic supplies such as shampoo, conditioner, toothpaste and toothbrush.

Megan looked at her registrar who was sitting opposite her, enjoying his coffee-break. 'You'll make an excellent father, Anthony.'

'I hope so. Now that it's so close, it all seems a bit daunting at times, although Lochie has promised to help me out and offer any advice I may need.'

'Isn't that just like Lochie?' Nicole grinned. 'Always helping out his mates. Oh, did you hear that last week, when old Alf went around to put up some more shelves in the closet at Lochie's house, he climbed up on another ladder, right beside old Alf, and helped him out.'

'He's very generous with his time,' Anthony agreed.

'When does Heather come? It can't be too much longer now.' Megan could have kissed Nicole for asking the question because it was the one she herself really wanted to know the answer to.

'Today. Now.' Anthony tapped his watch as though to prove his point. 'Lochie left for Sydney a few hours ago. Heather should be getting off the plane about now. I wonder if she flew all that way on her own?'

Megan frowned and checked the calendar on the wall.

'Today?' The word was out of her mouth before she could stop it. 'Uh…I thought it was next week.' Time had certainly flown and she wasn't sure how she could have lost track of the days. Or was she? She'd certainly spent more than a few nights thinking about Loughlin, punishing herself by remembering those spectacular kisses they'd shared and the inevitable outcome.

She'd had to focus twice as hard to get her evening paperwork done, had avoided him as best as possible at work and when she went to sleep, she would refuse to dream about him…although he was usually her first thought in the morning. That's where her mind had been—in schoolgirl fantasy land. It wasn't like her at all.

'Heather wasn't travelling on her own,' Megan supplied, knowing the answer to Anthony's question because Loughlin had mentioned it at some point. 'Her aunt and uncle are travelling with her.' She took her cup to the sink to wash it. 'I think I remember Loughlin saying that his sister and her husband were going to stay in Australia for three weeks to see a few of the sights. I know they're going to the Northern Territory to see Uluru and, of course, they'll spend some time in Sydney, taking in all the sights.'

'At least the weather's not going to be too bad for them. Early May can sometimes be rather wet but this year we're having quite a mild autumn,' Anthony added. 'You ready to do a final ward round check before calling it a night?'

'Let's get it done.' They headed to the wards and when Megan was satisfied that her patients were all settled for the evening, she headed to her office and collected a mound of paperwork. Amongst the papers she had to read tonight was an official offer from the community council, asking her to stay on as director for a further two-year contract at Kiama Hospital and Wellness Clinic.

She stopped off at Paula's restaurant to pick up something to eat and discovered that most people already knew about the offer. She should have guessed. Nothing secret ever went on in this town.

'There, now,' Paula remarked as Megan paid for her take-away dinner. 'Staying on here for a few more years will give you more than enough time to get to know gorgeous Dr McCloud even better.'

Unsure what to say, Megan merely nodded and smiled politely. She'd known since that first night when she and Loughlin had gone out for dinner that the tongues would wag, and she'd learned to take people's kindly meant interference with a grain of salt.

The gossip here was very different from that she'd encountered back in Sydney. In the hospital, she'd been on the receiving end of pitying looks and long sighs. The atmosphere had made her feel suffocated so she'd left. Now, in Kiama, there were no pitying looks and long, sad, sympathetic sighs. People were open and honest, encouraging her to get to know that dashing Dr McCloud.

'You've mellowed even more since he came long,' Mrs Newbold had told her just that morning. 'Having him around has been good for ya, girl. First Kiama works its magic on ya, stops your edges from being so sharp and now the handsome Scotsman is really smoothing them out.' Mrs Newbold had breathed in her oxygen as Megan had continued to assess her. 'He's a good one, young Megan. Don't let him go.'

Megan hadn't been at all sure what to say so she'd thanked Mrs Newbold for her kind words and continued with the check-up. And last week Loughlin had apologized—again. It was clear that he didn't like their present relationship and she knew she should just let go of the pain she'd felt at his rejection but it wasn't that easy.

She was a highly strung person. An over-achiever with anxiety who tended to over-think everything. Classic type A. Calvin hadn't wanted her and when she thought she'd dealt with that, when she'd thought that maybe she could take a step out of her comfort zone and be the easygoing and free person she desperately wanted to be, she'd been rejected yet again.

Calvin hadn't wanted her. Loughlin didn't want her either. The interesting fact was that she couldn't care less about Calvin and what he thought any more. Loughlin, however, was a completely different story. He was intelligent, fun to be around and a brilliant surgeon. She'd enjoyed the time they'd spent together and now, as crazy as it sounded, she was missing it.

Two days later, Megan heard her name being called as she came out of a shop. Turning, she saw Loughlin on the other side of the street, waving brightly at her. He was standing with some other people so, in order to be polite, she waved back.

They all crossed the road, heading in her direction, and where she'd been about to turn and walk in the other direction, it appeared he was intent on introducing her. There was Loughlin, another man and woman and a tall young girl she presumed was Heather. She had long blonde hair pulled back in a plait and the prettiest brown eyes, wide and expressive, like her father's.

'Is this Megsy, Da'?' Heather's accent wasn't as strong as her father's but still stood out in seaside Australia.

'Aye.'

With that, Heather stepped forward and wrapped her arms around a very surprised Megan. The embrace caught her completely off guard. 'Thank you. Thank you. *Thank you.* You are the bestest friend my da' could have had and did I say *thank you*?'

Megan patted the girl on the back, taken aback at the natural affection being given from someone she'd only just met. She looked at Loughlin in total confusion, her animosity melting away. 'What did I do?'

'The bed!' Father and daughter spoke in unison, although Heather's words were far more exuberant than Loughlin's.

'I *love* that bed. Thank you for insisting my da' buy it. It's the bomb!'

'Well…if it's the…bomb…' Megan got her tongue around the word, hoping she'd heard correctly. Teenage slang seemed to change every year and if you weren't a teenager, then you were seriously out of date. 'You're very welcome.'

'Let her go now,' Loughlin insisted, prising his daughter off Megan before giving her a 'what's a dad supposed to do?' type of shrug. Secretly, he was pleased at the way his daughter had catapulted her way directly through Megan's usual reserved exterior. Kids could do that. For adults, it was a lot harder. He'd had such difficulty these past few weeks, keeping his distance and making sure she accepted his apology. Hopefully, with Heather around, Megan might relax a little more around him.

He glanced surreptitiously at her, not having seen her for the past few days, and he couldn't get over how wonderful she looked.

Her blonde hair, which she usually kept clipped back for work, was now loose and framing her face, giving it a golden glow. She was dressed more casually than she usually was for work in a pair of comfortable jeans, a burgundy top and denim jacket.

Loughlin hadn't been able to stop thinking about her. Ever since that night…that night when he'd kissed her. He closed his eyes for a split second and the memory flooded over him. Her lips had been the sweetest, the most luscious he'd ever felt. The way she'd quivered slightly in his arms, the way her shyness had made way for passion. Oh, yes, kissing Megan Iris was something he wanted to do again—very much—and it was for that reason alone he'd forced himself to stay away from her.

He opened his eyes, pleased he could stand this close to her without having her back away. The pain and anguish he'd witnessed in her eyes that night had torn at his heart but he'd had to remain strong. He hadn't meant to hurt her but he had been so astounded at his own reaction that he'd handled the entire situation with all the grace and sympathy of an arrogant adolescent. He'd always been so guarded when it came to women, ensuring none of them got too close, that he remained in control and that Heather never got hurt.

Megan had blown all of that sky high because not only had

he discovered that he liked hanging out with her, chatting, discussing and generally just having fun, but he'd discovered he liked kissing her. Far too much. And he wanted more.

Even now, two weeks later, as he listened to her introduce herself to his daughter, saw Heather's wide smile of happiness, Loughlin wanted more. More intelligent conversation. More fun and definitely more kissing.

Yet he knew it was wrong and would only lead to a worse situation than he was in at present.

'Hello. I'm Georgie.' The woman beside Loughlin introduced herself and it was then that Loughlin realised he was still staring at Megan. He hoped his sister hadn't realised or she'd no doubt tease him mercilessly later.

'Sorry.' He snapped out of it. 'Bad manners and all that. Uh…Megsy, this is my sister Georgie and her husband Mike.'

Megan shook hands with them. 'It's great that you could come to Australia. Loughlin said you're staying for a few weeks, seeing some sights?'

'Aye.' Georgie nodded enthusiastically.

They chatted for a few minutes, Loughlin watching the way Megan interacted beautifully with his family. She was polite, friendly and was making conversation quite easily, asking Georgie about her children who, she was told, were busy studying for their university finals.

'Well, I'd better not keep you any longer. No doubt Loughlin wants to keep showing you around.' Megan took a small step to the side in an effort to indicate she was ready to move on. She'd been highly conscious of Loughlin watching her closely. His gaze had warmed her, causing her heart rate to increase along with her awareness of him. Thankful that she'd worked hard at controlling her natural reaction to his nearness—especially when they ended up side by side in an operating theatre, as had happened a few times—she hoped no one had noticed the slight tinge of pink which she'd felt colouring her cheeks.

'Och, goodness, hen. Doan't bother yerself about that. We're not in any rush,' Georgie offered, giving her brother a bit of a nudge. 'Right, Lochie?'

'Hmm?' Loughlin pulled his attention from looking at Megan and focused hard on what his sister was saying, unable to believe he'd been caught staring yet again. 'Aye. Right. What?'

'We're about to go and get something to eat,' Georgie continued. 'Why doan't you come with us, Megsy? Lochie wants us to eat a real Australian meat pie with tomato sauce instead of gravy! Have you ever heard such a daft thing?'

Megan glanced at Loughlin, wondering what he thought about his sister's invitation. 'I'd love to but I'm actually due to meet my brother down at the blow hole.'

'Really?' Loughlin's eyebrows hit his hairline. 'I didn't know your brother was in town.'

'You've been sort of busy the last few days and Jasper only called last night to say they were able to drive down,' she felt compelled to explain.

'Ah. Is this the new car?'

'It is. Needless to say, I'm quite excited.'

'Och, right.' Georgie nodded. 'Lochie told me how you two met. Quite a story.' She raised her eyebrows suggestively, her eyes as expressive as her brother's.

'Yes, well.' Megan tried not to feel flustered and decided the easiest thing to do was to make her escape. 'Anyway, it was lovely to meet you all and I hope you have a great holiday in Australia.' She smiled warmly at Georgie and Mike, all the time stepping around them, eager to have some distance between herself and Loughlin given that his nearness was having a devastating effect on her equilibrium.

It was insanely stupid that being so close to Loughlin made her heart pound wildly, her palms perspire and her knees go weak. That his scent brought back feverish memories of being pressed up against him, held firmly in his arms whilst his mouth plundered her own was enough of a reason to get moving as any.

'Is your brother from Sydney?' It appeared Georgie wasn't having a bar of allowing her to leave them and Megan idly wondered whether Loughlin had said something to his sister about what had gone on between them. Surely he hadn't mentioned the kiss? Oh, if he had, she'd die of embarrassment right here, right now. Then again, perhaps Georgie was picking up on the electrifying tension that seemed to exist between Megan and Loughlin…the tension that appeared to intensify every time they were close to each other.

'Ah…yes. Yes, he is,' she answered.

'We're heading there tomorrow so I'd love to chat with them about what to do and what to see first.' Georgie linked her arm through Megan's and pointed down the street. 'I presume you're heading this-a-way as I can see and smell the sea. The Pacific Ocean. How exciting.'

And soon Megan was introducing Loughlin and his clan to her own, with her four-year-old twin nieces, Lilly and Lola, instantly commandeering Heather's attention.

'They love older children,' Jennifer, Jasper's wife, told Georgie. Megan didn't miss the interested glances her brother was giving Loughlin. It was as though he was giving him the once-over, making sure this Scotsman was good enough for his sister. Whilst Megan hadn't said much to Jasper on the phone about Lochie, they were close enough that Jasper could read his sister like a book. So she stood there, in a state of repressed agitation, unsure what to do next whilst the two families seemed to hit it off without a care in the world.

'Care to go for a walk out to the blow hole?' Loughlin's voice was quiet beside her and Megan jumped, twirling around, surprised to find him behind her. Goose-bumps spread over her skin as his breath fanned her neck and a wave of excitement rushed through her. 'Or as close as the safety barriers will allow us,' he finished, giving her a wink.

'Uh…' Megan looked at his lips, finding them curved into a smile, before meeting his eyes. For a split second the atmosphere between them became incredibly intense. They were close to each other, their scents mingling with the sea breeze, their gazes locked, the tension in them both coiling to the point of no return.

His smile slowly began to disappear at the way she was looking at him. How was a man supposed to stay sane, to think clearly, when the woman he desired looked at him like she was now? It was impossible.

'Blow hole.' The words came out of her lips and for a moment Loughlin had no idea what she was on about.

'Hmm?' Then the fog began to clear as she eased back slightly, giving them both a bit of much-needed breathing space. 'Yes. That's right. Of course. The blow hole.' He shook his head as though to clear it, before taking a few steps towards the path that led to the phenomenal rock formation. 'We can start our truce on the way.'

'Our truce?'

'Yes. Didn't I mention I thought it might be a good idea to call a truce?'

'No. Actually, you didn't.'

'Och. How stupid of me. Some days I'm a right twit.'

'No argument from me,' she murmured, and was surprised when he burst out laughing, the sound causing her body to heat with warmth and flood with tingles.

'Oh, Megsy. I've missed ya.'

She wasn't at all sure what to say to that so instead decided to change the subject. 'How's Heather settling in? No jet-lag or anything?'

'She's fine is my girl. Fits in perfectly with the town.' He shook his head. 'She's only been here two days and loves it already. Although I have to say I cannae blame her. It's a great place.'

'It is at that.' They continued along the path and Megan frowned as she looked out towards the blow hole. 'Are those kids out there?'

The atmosphere she'd been trying to cope with due to Loughlin's close proximity turned instantly into concern as she pointed.

He looked in that direction and then frowned. 'Aye.'

'They've jumped the barrier!'

'Eejits.' They quickened their pace as they headed further towards the blow hole. 'Hey!' Loughlin called, and gestured to them. 'Get back.'

'It's no good, they can't hear you. The water crashing against the rocks is too loud.' Megan snapped open her phone and pressed the pre-set number for the police department. 'Gav. It's Megan. I've got teenagers out at the blow hole. They've jumped the fence.' She watched them as she spoke to the police officer.

'I think they have cameras,' Loughlin remarked as he peered more closely at them, still calling and gesturing for them to come in. By now other visitors to the area had started to notice the commotion and were all heading their way, coming for a look at the three people who were stupid enough to go against all the warning signs on the safety fence and put their lives at risk.

'They're obviously larking about but you and I both know how slippery those rocks are.' As Megan continued to speak, the blow hole erupted, sending its powerful salty spray showering into the air. 'Conditions are at least low,' she added as she finished her call to the police officer.

'Is he coming?' Loughlin asked.

'Yes. I've ordered an ambulance as well, just in case. Gav will contact the hospital to let them know to either expect casualties or else a person being brought in for blood-alcohol levels.'

'You think they're drunk?'

'Why else would they ignore all of the warning signs and—?'

An almighty, blood-curdling scream filled the air causing Megan and Loughlin to grip the edge of the safety barrier and watch in disbelief as one of the young men lost his footing and slipped. He grabbed at the air, struggling to remain upright, a look of absolute terror on his face as all his attempts resulted in nothing. He continued to fall at such an odd angle that Megan thought she saw him hit his head before he disappeared from view altogether. The camera he'd previously held so firmly now hurtled through the air, coming down to smash on the jagged rocks not too far from the blow hole.

The other two lads with him started to yell, to call his name, fear etched on their faces as they looked up at the spectators and started to call for help. Megan was glad that help was already on its way.

Jasper came running towards her. 'Megsy?' he called, concern plastered all over his face.

'I'm here.' She called and was soon enveloped in a large hug. 'I'm fine. Jasp, have you got a medical kit and some rope in your car?'

He nodded. 'I'll go get them.'

When Megan turned back to Loughlin to discuss what they should do next she was horrified to find he'd already climbed over the barrier—which came to just below her own shoulders—and was picking his way slowly and carefully across the rocks.

'What are you doing?' she yelled at him, her heart pounding wildly. 'Lochie. Wait.'

'It's fine. I just need to take a look.'

'Wait for the rope. Jasper's got some. He's getting it from his car. Please, Lochie,' she implored.

'I'm not going far, Megsy.' He smiled at her. 'I'll be back before you know it.'

She watched, her heart pounding wildly in her ears as he expertly picked his way over the rocks, telling the other boys to move back and stay where they were until further help arrived. Georgie came rushing over and stared out at her brother. Heather wasn't far behind.

'Da'? What are you doing?' she called to him, but he was out of hearing range.

'He'll be all right,' Megan said, hoping amongst hope that she was right.

'Och. I know that. He rock climbs all the time in Scotland.

They're bigger and scarier looking than this.' Heather waved Megan's concern away.

'And colder and wetter,' Georgie added.

'Good at abseiling, too, is my da'.' Heather spoke with pride.

'She's right. Lochie's a natural when it comes to nature.' Georgie smiled at her own words but when Megan looked at her, she saw a hint of concern in the woman's eyes. 'Has someone called for an ambulance or reinforcements of some kind?'

'It's been done.' Megan tore her gaze from Loughlin for a split second to see Jasper running towards her, medical kit in hand, a sturdy length of rope slung over his body. When she looked back at Loughlin, it was to find him making his way back to them, his steps quite sure and firm.

'He's slipped all the way into the hole. He's on the first shelf, though, which is better than being further down or we'd have had no hope. He's alert but rather dazed.'

'He's not unconscious?' Megan shook her head in disbelief. 'I thought I saw him hit his head on the way down.'

'He answered my calls.' Loughlin held out his hand for the rope as the sound of sirens filled the air. 'Ah…nice prompt service. Jinky. One of the advantages of living in a small town is that the emergency crews get here faster.' Whilst he spoke, he expertly tied the rope in a knot any sailor would have been proud of and attached one end to the railing before wrapping the other end around his waist.

Megan watched as though in slow motion as his firm, strong hands tied those knots, unsure why she was so concerned, so worried for his safety. She herself had been over the barrier before, albeit she'd been in a complete abseiling harness, performing a rescue very similar to the one they faced now, although that time the person they'd rescued hadn't answered their calls. She knew time was of the essence and when Loughlin had finished securing the rope to himself, she was surprised to find he didn't venture out again.

'What are you doing?'

'Waiting. I told you before, Megan Iris, that I was only taking a wee peek. I needed to figure out what had to happen next. If our friend Gav is almost here, he'll have the equipment we need. Right?'

'Right,' she replied, and found her heartbeat steadying to a more normal rhythm. Loughlin was going to wait. He wasn't going to put himself in danger, risk his own life to save someone else. He wasn't going to be a hero, and she was so relieved. She knew it was wrong to compare him to Calvin but she couldn't help it. Loughlin didn't have any of the arrogance and self-importance of her ex-fiancé.

When Gav arrived about five minutes later, he and Loughlin set about discussing the logistics of the situation. It was clear to everyone around just who was in charge of this rescue—the town's favourite Scotsman. He was amazing, going over in minute detail what they should do to proceed safely with the rescue.

She watched his mouth move, loving the lines and contours of them, remembering how those lips had felt pressed against her own, how they'd made her feel. She watched his eyes, so earnest, so deep in concentration, remembering how he'd looked at her as though she were the most beautiful woman to have walked the face of the earth. She watched his strong hands as he gestured and pointed, remembering how he'd brushed them across her cheek.

Her heart rate had increased again and she acknowledged that this time it had nothing to do with the rescue. It had nothing at all to do with anything surrounding them and everything to do with the fact that she cared deeply about him.

She had no idea how it had happened but the thought of him putting himself in danger had been enough to make her true feelings for him surge to the front. She'd promised herself when she'd moved here that she would never lie to herself again, that she'd never settle for second best. Loughlin was definitely *not* second best and admitting that she was one hundred per cent on the way to falling in love with him was definitely *not* lying to herself.

She blinked, shutting her eyes for a second, knowing she should focus on what was being discussed, but she couldn't. All that kept floating through her mind was that she was getting too close to him. Where she'd vowed never to make herself vulnerable to another man again, where she'd promised herself to always remain in control, where she'd never thought it possible for her heart to mend—it was irrelevant.

She was getting in deep with Loughlin McCloud and there didn't appear to be anything she could do about it—even if she wanted to!

CHAPTER EIGHT

Soon, Loughlin was harnessed up and ready to go. Gav was going out with him. The area had been roped off with yellow police tape but that didn't stop visitors, tourists and locals from watching at a distance.

Heather had gone with her aunt and uncle to a nearby park. Jennifer had also gone with the girls even though Megan had told her sister-in-law that her orthopaedic services might be required back at the hospital later on.

Jasper was monitoring the two other lads who had seen their friend fall, concerned for the trauma they might be experiencing. Megan was fitting herself into a harness, knowing she would be needed.

'It's all right,' Loughlin had protested. 'I think Gav and I can handle it. No need to make a palaver out of it.'

'I'll palaver you into the middle of next week, Dr McCloud,' Megan warned him. Loughlin watched the way her fingers expertly attached the abseiling ropes and realised that she'd done this before.

'I just don't think it's worth putting you in danger.'

'According to you, every thing is going to be fine.'

'It is. So there's no ne—'

Megan reached up and put her fingers across his mouth. 'Shut it, Lochie.'

He stared at her for a moment, seeing the determination in her eyes flicker with a hint of desire as she realised just how near they were to each other. He also saw concern and realised she was as worried about his safety as he was about hers.

'OK.' He waited for Megan to secure a rescue kit to her chest, identical to the one strapped to his own, before they pulled on protective goggles and abseiling gloves and carefully made their way over to the blow hole.

'At least the swell is low…for the moment,' she commented. It had seemed like an age since the accident had first happened when in reality it had only been about fifteen minutes or so. Safety precautions, however, were paramount because they wouldn't do anyone any good if any of the rescuers were to slip and fall due to being too hasty.

When they were as close as they could be to the entrance of the blow hole, the water came up and sprayed them, wetting them through, both Loughlin and Megan gasping as the cold water seeped through their clothes against their skin. Gav was lying down on his stomach at the mouth of the hole, shining a searchlight down onto the teenager, keeping him as calm as possible.

'What took you both so long?' the policeman asked, grinning at the two doctors.

'Traffic,' Loughlin answered, deadpan. His answer made Megan smile, made her body relax just that little bit more so the tension wasn't as strong as it had been before.

Megan and Loughlin lay down on their stomachs alongside Gav, peering down into the hole, the rush of water quite loud beneath them. 'Bloke's name is Barry. He's nineteen, almost twenty. It's pretty hard to hear and you can only talk at certain times.' Gav stopped speaking and averted his head in anticipation of the water that was about to shoot up at them. Loughlin and Megan did the same.

When it had passed, Loughlin looked into the hole. 'Barry? I'm Lochie. We'll have you out in a jiffy.' With the powerful searchlight they could see that Barry had somehow managed to get himself to a small ledge close to the bottom of the hole and was hanging on for dear life. It was clear there was no way he would be able to tie a rope around his own waist. He was becoming exhausted far too quickly with the effort of simply hanging on for his life.

'OK,' he yelled back.

'I'll go down,' Loughlin said. 'If we can secure the rope around him, we can pull him out.'

Gav nodded. 'Best way. Straightforward.'

Megan looked down into the hole again and shook her head. 'You can't do it. It's—' Before she could say another word, they all ducked their heads, ready for the next lot of spray to shower into the air above them.

'*You* can't go down. I won't let you.' Loughlin's words were strong, his accent rich and deep. Through her safety goggles, Megan could see a hint of veiled panic in his eyes. Did that mean he cared? More than he'd previously let on? She brushed the thought aside but was determined to take it out later and examine it more closely. For now, she needed to concentrate.

'It's not a matter of letting me, Lochie.' She pointed down the hole. 'You won't fit. As slim and as tall as you are, you're not the right shape to fit through that hole.'

'She's right, mate,' Gav chipped in. 'Besides, Megan's already been down before. She knows what to expect.'

They started getting her ready, ensuring she was completely secure. Helmet with light, strong gloves and extra safety goggles for Barry. When she was ready, Loughlin looked into her eyes and gave her a crooked smile.

'Take it easy, Megsy,' he said, before winking. Her heart filled with warmth at the gesture and with renewed determination that this rescue was going to go exactly as they'd planned she swung herself around with her legs dangling down into the hole, her abseiling rope falling down into the abyss. She braced herself, waiting for the next blast from the blow hole, knowing she needed to descend at a rapid rate in order to get to Barry.

As soon as it had passed by her, before the spray from above had come to settle down on them, she shifted her hand, feeding the rope through as she headed into the darkness. Even though she had her helmet light and Gav had a searchlight above, it was dark, damp and downright freaky being in this hole which had been carved out through generations of erosion.

'Barry?' she called as she neared where he was.

'Hello?'

Megan moved her head to the left and spotted him—the light from her helmet shining into his scared face as he clung to the rock face for dear life.

'Barry. I'm Megan.' She locked off her rope so she was all but sitting in mid-air. She could hear the rush of the water building below them. 'As soon as the next one goes up, we need to move fast. They'll send down a rope and I'll need your help to secure it around you.'

'It's coming. It's coming.' Barry closed his eyes, clenched his hands tightly as he did his best to flatten himself to the rock face. Megan could hear the hysteria in his voice and knew she needed to go slowly and carefully if she was going to get them both out in one piece. However, right now Barry was correct and she manoeuvred herself to the opposite side of the rock face and found firm handholds, flattening herself as best she could.

The roar of the water started to build and then with a powerful force it rushed up past them, drenching them once more. The instant it passed she pulled a pair of spare safety goggles from the pack strapped to her chest and swung over so she was next to Barry. 'Let's get these on you first.' It was hard work with her thick wet gloves and the fact that Barry wasn't letting go of his handholds for anything. By the time she had them in place, there was only enough time for her to return to her former position and wait for the next blast to be delivered. She was, however, grateful that the tide was low because this would have been nigh impossible later in the day.

'Send the rope,' she called as loudly as she could, and in the next instant Loughlin lowered the rope for Barry. Megan was able to find a safe spot next to Barry, although it wasn't as sheltered as the previous one, and the instant the water blasted past them she immediately looped the rope around Barry's waist. 'Let me get it past,' she said, her tone brooking no argument. The young man was scared, tired and bordering on hysteria. He'd flattened himself so tightly against the rock face that she couldn't get the rope all the way round his body. The water was building up once more below them.

'Barry, let me get it round you,' she ordered. 'Once it's round you, we can start pulling you out.'

'No. No. I'm going to fall.'

'You are not going to fall.' The water was coming. 'Let me get the rope round you.' Her tone was still firm and direct. *'Now!'* As she barked the order, he arched his stomach so she could slip the rope round. Holding both ends, she resumed her secure position, almost letting go of the rope as the blasts seemed to be getting stronger.

Megan hoped that wasn't the case and merely the fact that she herself was starting to become slightly fatigued, but she knew she had enough reserves to get her through. They were so close to success she wasn't about to let it all slip away now. Besides, she had Loughlin waiting for her up at the surface. She could hear him calling down words of encouragement and his lilting tones gave her strength. He was waiting for her.

When she could, she secured the rope tightly, fitting it beneath Barry's armpits. 'After the next one, I need you to let go of the wall so you can be pulled up.'

'No. No. I'm going to fall. I know it. I'm going to die.'

'You are *not* going to die. Do you hear me? Not going to happen. We've come this far, Barry. You can do this.'

'I'm hurt.'

'I know. I can see your legs are hurt. I can see the bruises and scratches and the sooner you're out, the sooner we can do something about it. I need you to trust me. I need you to trust those men up top who are waiting to pull you out as soon as I give the signal.'

Barry thought about her words, pondering them whilst the water built beneath them. 'What's the signal?' he finally asked.

Megan smiled as she prepared herself for the next onslaught. The panic had started to subside—just a little—from Barry's voice. She'd successfully managed to get through to him. 'I yell, "Ready."'

'That's it?'

'Yep. Simple and straightforward. Works every time. Trust me.' Megan held onto the rock face, as did Barry. 'Right. We need to work fast. You need to practise letting go, Barry. Trust the rope. It will take your weight.' She looked up and saw Loughlin leaning over so much that his upper torso was dangling into the hole. 'Almost ready. After the next one, pull.'

'Aye, aye, Captain Megsy,' he called back, his words echoing around them. Megan couldn't help but grin.

'See?' she said to Barry. 'We'll be as safe as houses.'

'What? What does that mean?'

'Well…it means we'll be super-safe. Quite frankly, I didn't want to say that we'd be as right as rain.'

Barry smiled at her and she knew in that instant that everything was going to be just fine. The pressure had been lifted, the tension was returning to a more normal level and Barry was starting to believe he *would* get out of this hole.

When they were ready, she gave the signal and watched as Barry was hauled out quite quickly. He grunted and groaned a little on the way up as he swung around a bit, but just as the next blast started to make its way up the hole, she saw Loughlin grab his hand. She flattened herself against the rock face, hopefully for the last time, and when she looked up again, it was to see only sunlight. Barry had made it.

She had to wait for three more blasts to pass before Loughlin's words echoed down to her. 'Ready to get you out of there, Megsy. OK?'

'Aye, aye, Captain Lochie,' she called back, exhaustion beginning to creep into her tone. His laughter floated down to her and that glorious sound gave her strength to hang on for just that little bit longer.

When at last she was within reach of the top, Loughlin's strong arms reached down and took her hands, pulling her higher. The blow hole was about to perform its magic again and he quickly hauled her against him. In the next instant she was lying flat along the length of his body as the spray washed over them.

She sagged against him in utter relief, not caring about anyone or anything else except for Loughlin's strong arms around her, holding her securely to him as though he was never going to let her go. She didn't care who was watching. She didn't care if she stayed where she was for the next hour. All energy seemed to have drained from her the instant he'd pulled her into his arms. She was safe. She was with Loughlin. He would protect her.

'Trauchled?' His voice was a deep rumble beneath her ear which was pressed on his chest. When she didn't answer, Loughlin smiled, loving the feel of her this close. 'Sorry. Forgot to switch on my universal translator. Are you totally exhausted or can you move? Not that I'm trying to rush you or anything. I'm quite fine.' And he was.

He was enjoying holding her in his arms and was overcome with the sensation that he never wanted to let her go. It seemed like an age since he'd held her, since he'd kissed her, and although he knew putting distance between them was the right thing to do, he couldn't deny how good it felt to have an excuse to have her this near.

Megan tried to speak. It didn't work. She tried to nod her head. That didn't work either. The adrenaline surge she'd had down the blow hole, concentrating on getting Barry out whilst gripping to that rock face, had totally disappeared and in its place was complete lethargy and fatigue.

'Mmm,' she finally managed, and her reward for even attempting to answer his question was one of Loughlin's throaty laughs, which set her body tingling in a floating, relaxed way. Quite a few more bursts of spray washed over them before Loughlin told her it was time to move.

'You're soaked, love. We need to get you dry.' With that, he somehow shifted her and before she knew it she was being carefully led over the uneven rocky surface, Loughlin's arms still firmly around her, supporting her, keeping her close.

'Barry?' she managed to ask once she was over the barrier and could collapse in a heap. The wetness of her soaked clothes was now starting to affect her, her teeth beginning to chatter. Someone put a blanket around her shoulders and she pulled it tighter, only then realising that her gloves had been removed. She couldn't remember that happening.

'He's fine,' Gav told her. 'Your brother's looking after him.'

Megan relaxed, knowing Barry was in good hands. 'Lochie?' She opened her tired eyes and looked around for him. She couldn't see him anywhere and she tried to sit up straight, squinting to try and find him. He didn't appear to be in the immediate vicinity and she suddenly felt panic begin to rise within her. 'Lochie? Where is he?' Had he slipped? Had he fallen? The last thing she remembered was his arms firmly around her and she wanted them around her now. No. She *needed* them around her now, *needed* the comfort and strength she drew from him. 'Lochie?' Megan raised her voice, the urgency now evident.

'I'm here. I'm here.' From nowhere, he appeared by her side. 'Everything's jinky. Everything's all right, Megsy. Rest now, darlin'.'

'Hold me?'

Her request was a whimper and Loughlin couldn't believe she was letting him see her this vulnerable, showing him this softer side of her and allowing him to comfort and soothe her. Gone was the woman he'd thought was as prickly as an echidna and in her place was a woman who needed him. He gathered her close without another word.

'Don't leave me,' she murmured, her eyes closed, the panic gone from her voice, her body relaxed against his.

'Nay.' Loughlin held her, rubbing her arms, warming her up until it was time for her to go to the hospital. He checked in with his sister to make sure Heather was all right.

'Stay with Megsy as long as you need to,' Georgie told him. 'We can get back to your place without a bother so don't you go fretting.'

He was pleased he could be there to support Megan and by the time she'd changed into some dry clothes and sipped a warm cup of sugary tea, she was feeling much better.

'You don't have to stick around, Loughlin,' she told him after he'd made sure she'd drunk the entire cup full of the sweetened tea he'd prepared. 'Go. Be with your family. Jasper can take me home.' They were in her office, somewhere where she felt comfortable, somewhere where she hoped to gather a semblance of control. She was sitting behind her desk and he was leaning against the edge, too close for her comfort.

Loughlin ignored her words. 'Quite a doctor is your brother. Highly impressive.'

Megan's smile was immediate. 'We're all very proud of Jasper.'

'I watched him work when I went to check on Barry's progress and he's got all the staff organised as well as the patient ready for transfer to Sydney. Has he worked here before?'

'Not *worked* exactly but he's been here enough times that the staff know him and, of course, a few of them have worked with him in Sydney so it's like he's amongst old friends.'

'Add to that fact that his sister is director of the hospital so people will want to jump when he asks them to. They'd do it for no other reason than to make sure their jobs are secure in case he reports back to you on their conduct.'

Megan was about to contradict him, to let him know it wasn't like that, when she noticed that tell-tale twinkle in his eyes that indicated he was teasing. Was this his way of helping her not to feel so self-conscious about what had transpired between them at the blow hole?

She'd been quietly embarrassed when she'd finally changed into warm clothes and begun feeling more like herself. She remembered all too clearly the way Loughlin had held her, the way he'd protected her, the way she'd begged him to stay with her. Poor man. He must think she was completely desperate. She lifted her chin, determined to get rid of those thoughts and regain control over her wayward emotions, especially where Loughlin McCloud was concerned.

'Well, if that's what you think, then you'd better make sure *you* do as you're told to ensure *you* impress the director adequately enough to secure your *own* job.'

She'd meant her words to be delivered in the same teasing manner as Loughlin's but all she succeeded in doing was to make matters more intense. Loughlin shifted from his perch, leaning forward a little more, bringing his face dangerously close to her own. Immediately, her breathing increased, her senses became heightened and her lips parted as their eyes met and held.

'If that's the case, Dr Edwards…' He drawled her name as though it were the softest of caresses. His voice as smooth as silk. 'You had better tell me how I may impress you.'

They were close, so close their breaths began to mingle as the tension continued to heighten. Megan was sure that between them they'd be able to generate so much power they could light up the whole of Kiama. The more time she spent with him, the greater the effect, especially as she'd already realised she was in real danger of falling in love with him.

But she'd talked herself out of being in love with one man in the past and she could do it again. Fantasising about Loughlin was going to bring her nothing but heartache and she'd had enough of that already.

'I don't…' she breathed out, trying not to be affected by him '…think this is a good idea.'

'I disagree.'

'You didn't think it was a good idea last time we were this close.'

'You're wrong. I thought it was *too* good an idea.'

'But that would imply that…you *liked*…er…' She faltered, unable to concentrate clearly because of his nearness.

'Kissing you? Och, aye, Megsy. I liked it far too much.'

'But we can't.'

'I ken that but it doesn't mean I don't want to.'

'This is crazy,' she whispered, her heart pounding wildly.

'Aye.'

'Lochie.' She breathed his name, wanting him to kiss her, knowing that would provide far more warmth to her cold body than the tea he'd made her drink.

'I like it when you call me that,' he murmured, his deep words only continuing to intensify the atmosphere between them. 'I like the way my name sounds coming from your sweet lips.'

'Lochie,' she repeated, pleased she could affect him as powerfully as he affected her. 'Kiss me.'

'I want to. I really do.' He was close, so close that if Megan simply leaned forward and upwards, their mouths would come into contact, and although they were both acknowledging it was what they wanted, there was still the smallest hint of rational thought between them.

'I've thought of you so much, wanted to kiss you so much. A man shouldn't be denied the most glorious pair of lips, the most intense sensations, the most powerful reaction when he's once savoured it. It's not right to deny ourselves. Is it?'

Was that really how he saw her? Megan had been under the impression that he hadn't been affected by her at all, that she was just another woman, there for him to flirt with, to charm, to kiss. He'd said their last kiss had been a mistake and she wondered at the burning need within her to have him repeat that mistake again and again and again. She'd deal with the consequences later. Right now all she could think about was the way he made her feel at this moment.

'Lochie.' His name was barely a whisper coming from unmoving lips. She couldn't disagree with what he'd said and where she'd always been such a logical thinker throughout her entire life, this was one time she didn't want logic to have any part in what was between them.

'Why? Tell me why I *shouldn't* be kissing you every chance I get?' His words were thick, laced with a deep, abiding need.

'Because I lose control. When you kiss me, I forget everything and that scares me. I'm always in control and when you…' She breathed out, trying to control her reaction to him so she could at least get these words out. 'When you're near, when you touch me, when you kiss me, the world slips away and I am floating on air. On feathers. On pillows. On feathers on pillows on air.' Her words were becoming more urgent as she tried to convince a man who desperately wanted to kiss her—to actually do it. 'I feel so wonderful.'

'I keep dreaming about you,' he whispered, and a new flood of tingles buzzed through her body at his words. 'Wondering. Wanting. Waiting.'

'So you…you find me attractive, then?' As soon as the words were out of her mouth she closed her eyes, not wanting to hear the answer but at the same time desperate to know the truth.

'Find you attractive? Megsy, you put my body into an uproar just by being in the same room as me. Och, aye, lassie. I find ye very attractive.'

She opened her eyes, looking intently into his. 'You do?' It was what she needed to hear and to now know that she was so desirable to him, that he dreamt of her, that he wanted her so badly that it was forcing him to break one of his own rules, made Megan feel incredibly special. When she'd been left at the altar, she'd thought that Calvin had broken her heart for ever but now she knew that wasn't the case. Now she knew she could love Loughlin—strange but true—yet that didn't mean her heart wasn't in danger.

'Lochie. I am not a patient woman and whilst I'm loving what you're saying, astonished at hearing your words, to know that you dr-dream about me, it's enough to set me on fire.' She looked deeply into his eyes as she spoke. 'I know there's turmoil. I know we both want to ignore this thing between us but not now. Not here. We can't ignore it any more. I need you.'

And he realised she did…but for how long? He'd been cast aside too many times before. He'd fallen for his ex-wife's lies time and time again until he'd finally learned his lesson—the hard way. Women, especially women such as Megan, who were so intelligent yet so closed off to the world around them, intrigued him so intensely it was no wonder he was falling for her. If he gave in to the desire to kiss her lips, lips which would connect with his with the slightest forward movement from either of them, would he only be setting himself up for a greater heartache? Setting *both* of them up for heartache?

'Nay. I cannae…'

Her heart began to plummet at his words. *No!* she wanted to scream. He was so close. So close, so near, so necessary. Her emotions were as taut as a drum and she was sure they were about to snap at any second.

Loughlin's breathing increased, as did his need for her. 'I cannae not kiss you.'

With that, he leaned forward. The instant she heard his words, felt his movement, she leaned up, lacing her hands around his neck, her fingers plunging into his rich, spiky hair.

Their mouths came together with such a fierce intensity that it startled them both. It was as though abstaining from kissing for the past two and a half weeks had only made the attraction which existed between them far more powerful than either one realised.

She was entering uncharted territory and she didn't care. Not now. She didn't care about anything except this one moment in time. Impulsiveness was not something she ever gave in to but here she was, doing what she wanted to do when she wanted to do it. Her breath caught in the back of her throat as his lips stilled momentarily over hers, as though he wanted to prolong the sensation, commit it to memory.

It was strange yet sensually delightful to have their mouths fused together without any movement at all, as though being still, simply enjoying this rapturous moment, gave their other senses time to catch up.

'Megsy. Are you ready to—?' Jasper burst into her office, causing Loughlin and Megan to wrench themselves from their sensual bubble. 'Oh. I'm so sorry.' Jasper immediately turned and walked out, closing the door firmly behind him.

Megan looked from her closed door to Loughlin. He'd taken quite a few steps away from her and she could tell by the set of his jaw that they weren't about to pick up where they'd left off.

'Family,' he tried to joke, but even to his own ears, his word sounded hollow. He took another step backwards, his eyes intent on hers, his heart pounding wildly. That had been the most amazing kiss of his life. So gentle. So alluring. So completely sensual. He knew it wasn't just the act of pressing his lips to Megan's luscious ones that had made him tremble. It was the realisation he'd come to.

He might have fallen in love with his boss!

CHAPTER NINE

WHAT was he supposed to do?

Loughlin stood looking out of the living-room window into the dark of night. It was one week since he'd kissed Megan and he'd been asking himself the same question ever since. What had he done? He couldn't possibly be in love with the woman. He hardly knew her.

He ran a hand through his hair and wasn't surprised to find it not so steady. Thoughts of Megan often made him react in ways he wasn't used to. She was quite a woman, he could at least admit that much. She was so highly intelligent he sometimes felt like going back to university to study some more just so he could keep up with her.

He liked it when she talked about their work, about operating techniques and new equipment coming out on the market. Usually it was after ward round or in the tearoom and usually there were other people around, taking the opportunity to ask her questions. He wondered why she hadn't gone into a different speciality.

Then he realised it was no doubt because she didn't have the arrogance required. He smiled to himself, recalling a conversation they'd had previously. He remembered the day he'd stopped to help her with her car. It hadn't been that long ago yet it seemed like for ever.

She'd looked so beautiful that day, so haughty, so determined to fix the car herself, so eager to keep him at a distance. She'd looked beautiful every day since and he'd been surprised at her uncertainty the other day. Had she honestly thought that he'd stopped kissing her that first time because he thought she was unattractive? It appeared so and it also told him a lot about her previous relationship.

No. He'd stopped kissing her because she was addictive and he didn't need to be addicted to anything, especially not another career-woman. Granted, even though she was dedicated to her career, she was completely different from Bonnie.

For the past week things had been…interesting between them. They'd both been polite, happy. Sometimes overly happy as though they were trying to cover up the indecision that appeared to be their confused relationship. Neither of them seemed to know what to do next and whilst Loughlin was bothered by it, he could see it was driving Megan almost crazy. He smiled at the thought. She was certainly a woman who liked to be in control but he admired her for trying to take a step into the unknown.

At least a thousand times each day he'd had to resist the temptation to kiss her. To do that would get them nowhere…except to perhaps lead them both down a path they might not mentally be ready to tackle. Physically…well, that was definitely another issue. There was no denying that in the chemistry department the pheromones were working overtime and that was why it was difficult to keep his distance.

If they found themselves alone in a room, they would talk about Heather or their work or even sometimes just discuss different books they'd read. In short, the more time he spent with her, the more he liked her, and although he'd kept reminding himself to keep looking for flaws, something that would help break this hold she appeared to have over him, he was having trouble coming up with any.

Sure, she was highly strung and a few times he'd caught her controlling her breathing, making him a little concerned that something might be wrong but he had no idea what. Tension? Stress? Anxiety? She wouldn't be the first medic to suffer from the pressures of the job and, being such a perfectionist, he knew most of the pressure would come from no one else but herself. She wanted to do her job well and he couldn't fault that.

In short, Megan was everything he was looking for in a woman and yet there were huge barriers between them, hurdles that needed to be jumped. The main problem was, the hurdles were so big he wasn't sure he'd be able to get over them. It was the fact that Megan *was* everything he was looking for that made him so tentative and confused.

The phone rang and he rushed to pick it up in case it woke Heather. Perhaps it was Megan? Perhaps she needed him for an emergency? His heartbeat increased at the thought of seeing her. He so desperately wanted to yet at the same time he wanted to put as much distance between them as possible. 'Lochie,' he said into the receiver.

'Wee one.' Georgie's sweet voice came down the line.

'Hey, there.' His heartbeat slowed to a more normal rhythm. It was just his sister, calling him the nickname he'd been given as a young boy. 'What's going on?'

'Och, not much. We've just returned from having dinner with Megan's brother and his family. My goodness, those girls are a handful. Completely gorgeous but a handful.'

'No doubt. So how are they?'

'Good. We discussed you.'

'Oh?' Loughlin wasn't at all sure how he felt about that. Was that a good thing? *Should* they be discussing him? Was there anything to discuss?

'Aye. Jasper seems to think there will be wedding bells soon.'

Loughlin closed his eyes, knowing exactly why Jasper was thinking that way. 'And?'

'And I think so, too. I like Megan. She's lovely. Perfect for you.'

He opened his eyes and frowned into the phone. 'You hardly

spent any time with her, Georgie. You saw her briefly the day after the blow-hole incident in the grocery store.'

'And we had a lovely chat. Did ye ken her eyes light up when she says your name?'

'They do?'

Georgie laughed. 'She's a good person, Lochie. Sometimes it can only take a moment to realise that and I think things are going to work out.'

'Why? Because her eyes light up when she says my name?' There was a hint of disbelief in his tone but part of him was desperate for some of his sister's optimism.

'That's part of it. I think she's nothing like Bonnie and I hope you're not comparing them.' His sister, who had always been his confidante, paused. 'I know ye like her, Lochie. It was evident just watching the two of you interact the other day. And she likes you. So what's the problem?'

Loughlin began to pace the floor, not really looking where he was going and not really caring. 'Too many to mention. We've both been hurt before.'

'I know. Jasper mentioned Megsy's aborted wedding. That cannae have been easy for her.'

'It wasn't.'

'And we all know how many times you've been stabbed by Bonnie's stilettos. The point is, for both of ye, those things are in the past. They're over. They're done with. You need to move on, move forward. Get on with your life.'

'I am which is why I uprooted Heather and moved to Australia.'

'And met Megan.'

'You think this is…meant to be?'

'I do, but we both know I'm a hopeless romantic at heart.'

'Aye. Look, there's no denying that I like Megsy. Heck, I even might love her but that doesn't mean things are going to work out. It's not as though a fairy godmother is going to fly down, wave her magic wand and, *poof*, everything is perfect. My heart has been torn, twisted and tortured enough. I'm not going to risk it again.'

'Why not?'

'What if she hurts me? What if I declare my feelings for her and she rejects me? I can't go through that again. Besides, I have Heather to think about. Heather must come first.'

'Don't go using that girl as an excuse.' Georgie's tone was stern and he realised she sounded like his mother. 'Ye deserve happiness, Lochie, and if that's with Megan, you need to grab it with both hands and hold on and never let go. Plus, although Heather is a well-adjusted pre-teen, there are going to be a lot of times in the coming years when she's going to need another woman to talk to. Now, ye ken we're always here for ye both but we're also going to be half a world away. Although, I must say, the little I've already seen of this country I love. Wouldn't mind moving here myself.'

'Glad to hear it.' Loughlin was still pondering his sister's earlier words. He knew she wasn't telling him to get married just so Heather could have a mother figure around. He knew she wasn't telling him to rush into anything without thinking things through. He knew she was telling him to be careful not to lock himself up too tightly.

'It may be time.' Georgie's words were soft. 'Ye need to take a step out of the darkness into the light.'

'What if she does reject me? What if she doesn't want what I want? She's a career-woman, Georgie. She's talking about not even staying in Kiama when her contract expires. She doesn't want to stay in one place. She wants to move, to do new things, to… Oh, I don't know what she wants but it isn't to stay in town, to put down roots, to get married, to have a family. She's a surgeon first and foremost and I cannae see her changing any of that.' He stopped walking and stared out into the night yet again. Why weren't the answers to his many questions just floating around out there, waiting for him to claim them?

'How do ye know what she wants unless ye ask her, eh? Maybe she's willing to do all of those things but thinks that you don't want her so she'll just move on with her life—without you. We women are strange and complicated creatures, wee one, and sometimes we need to be given a completely different option to consider.'

'Hmm.'

'Sounds as though you're the one considering.'

He could hear the smile in Georgie's voice. 'I'd better let you go. Call me when you get to Uluru so I know you're safe.'

'Will do. Love to Heather…oh, and to you.'

'Right back at you, big sister.' He rang off, his thoughts whirring even faster than before. Just because he'd realised he was in love with Megsy, it didn't mean they would end up happily ever after. He wasn't as naive as he'd been when he'd first married Bonnie.

He went and checked on Heather, standing by her bed just listening to her breathe. The two of them had worked hard at making their life as smooth as possible and to add someone else to the mix could be disastrous. Heather must be protected.

He'd noticed her spending some time with Megan during the week, especially as Megan had offered her office for Heather to do her homework in. A few times when he'd been ready to leave, he'd found the two of them talking, sometimes laughing together. It warmed his heart that Heather had bonded so easily with Megsy but at the same time warning bells had started to ring. He didn't want Heather getting too close to Megan just in case things didn't work out…because at the moment he wasn't sure they would. He was a dad who needed to protect his baby girl.

Heather still looked tiny in that huge bed and he couldn't help the smile that touched his lips as he recalled Megan being so adamant that she wasn't going to get on to help him test it out. In hindsight, he realised she'd been right. Even back then, the tension between them had been strong. Now, after the rescue at the blow hole and the events that had followed, the tension was almost at breaking point.

In a few months' time, Megan would no doubt be gone, leaving Kiama for somewhere different. The thought brought many mixed emotions. He wondered what life in the seaside town would be like without her around and all he could see before him was darkness. If she left, she'd take the light with her and then what?

At the same time, he knew if she did leave, it might be better for all concerned. He could protect his heart and Heather, and Megan could go and find whatever it was she was looking for.

Loughlin headed back to the living room and stood at the window again.

What was he supposed to do?

One week after the blow-hole rescue, Megan was standing at her living-room window looking out into the night—only one thought on her mind.

What was she supposed to do?

She hadn't believed her own emotions when she'd discovered she'd fallen in love with Lochie. It wasn't in her plan and she was a woman who always stuck to the plan. She liked things to be organised, to be structured and to be within her control.

Loughlin didn't promote any of those things. He made her feel so out of control, so spontaneous and free. Most of all, she realised it was OK to be that way. She'd liked the few times she'd stepped outside that very comfortable comfort zone she inhabited but each time it seemed to bring more confusion, more questions and even a bit of pain.

She couldn't be in love with a man she barely knew. Could she? And if she was, what would happen when she found out more about him? Would she fall out of love with him? Would that love only grow deeper?

Everything with Calvin had been so neatly organised and

structured and she now knew that had been because Calvin was similar to her. There had been no real dramas in their relationship, not until he'd left her at the altar. Yet with Loughlin there had been one drama after another from the instant they'd met. He made her feel far more vulnerable and scared than she'd ever been before. He was making her question herself, too. Not directly but emotionally. Was cutting herself off from him what she needed to do in order to ensure her heart didn't get pulverised again? Would it preserve her? Did she want to be preserved?

Closing her eyes for a moment, she shook her head. Her thoughts were only going round in circles at this point and she realised she needed to talk to someone. In the next instant she had the phone to her ear and was listening to it ring.

'Mum?'

'Megsy. What a lovely surprise. How are you, darling?'

She quickly went through the niceties with her mother, checking up on her brother and his family to ensure everyone was healthy. They talked about her new car and hospital life, Megan wondering how on earth she could swing the conversation around to the topic of her confusing love life. She need not have worried.

'Did you know that your Loughlin's sister and her husband have just been to Jasper's for dinner? We met them and they're such lovely people. Georgie's accent is very strong but the way she talks about that brother of hers, well, you can tell that she thinks the world of him.'

'Yes. They seem very close.'

'That's good. It's good for family to be close. To be able to tell each other things.' Iris's words were highly pointed. 'Such as whether they're dating a colleague who just happens to be from Scotland.'

'What have you heard?'

'Nothing. Well, not really. From the general direction of the conversation, it appears both Jasper and Georgie are of the understanding that you and Loughlin are a couple.'

Megan closed her eyes and shook her head. She knew it was because Jasper had walked in on them kissing and had therefore jumped to conclusions. He hadn't broached the subject with her when she'd seen him before they'd left Kiama to return to Sydney and she'd hoped she was off the hook. It appeared not.

'Megan Iris?'

Her eyes snapped open at her mother's tone. 'Yes?'

'Are you? Are you dating this Scotsman?'

'No.'

'Oh. Then why do you presume your intelligent brother would think otherwise?'

Megan sighed. 'Because he caught us kissing. Oh, Mum. I don't know what to do. I'm so confused. More confused than I've ever been before.' The words tumbled over each other so quickly she had to gasp for breath. 'Lochie and I aren't dating but, Mum, I think I've fallen in love with him!'

'Love?'

'Yes. I know. Ridiculous, isn't it? I mean, I hardly know him but he's incredible and smart and funny and he's always making me laugh and he's sweet and sexy and has the most amazing smile and I feel completely at ease when I'm with him. Well, when he's not tying me up in knots with the way he makes my heart race every time I look into his eyes. And his voice.' She sighed. 'Oh, he has the most amazing voice and I love listening to him talk and when I think about him, I don't get the chest pains and I feel like I just want to lie back and listen to him talk all day long. And he's funny—'

'So you've said.'

'Except when he totally frustrates me and sometimes I just want to knock him over the head with a book or something. And then we're kissing and then I'm mad at him and then I decide I need to mellow out and then I find I'm in love with him and then he's kissing me and then he's not sure what he wants and the whole thing is a confusing mess.'

'Sounds like it.'

'Mum. I don't know what to do. What should I do?'

'Oh, Megsy. I can't tell you what to do. You're a grown woman. I do think that leaving Sydney was the right thing for you and Kiama has certainly helped you. You've told me before that your chest pains aren't as bad and it's great that Loughlin helps you but, darling, you can't rely on him to just come along and fix your life.'

'That's not what I want.'

'Isn't it? Are you really in love with him or are you just infatuated by the way he has you reacting? You're experiencing new emotions, you're thinking outside your usual box and that's all great, but is it gratitude you feel for this man?'

Megan started to bristle at her mother's words. 'No. No. Well, of course I'm grateful that he stopped and helped me that first day, and having him at the hospital has helped make my working life easier.'

'Well, there you are, then.'

'But I feel happy when I'm with him.'

'And yet he frustrates you?'

'Yes, but only when he's being obtuse, and no doubt I frustrate him, too. We're very similar in a lot of respects and very different as well. He's been through a bad marriage and we all know my sad little story and it's as though together we've found some common ground, an area where we both understand and appreciate each other's pain.'

'A bond has formed.'

'Yes.'

'But is it really a bond of love? One that you can build a solid foundation on? Megan, I'm not meaning to be horrible or unsupportive, darling, but I just don't want to see you hurt again. Calvin was never any good for you and I don't know if this man is either. His sister certainly seems nice but that's no reason to jump into a relationship with him…not when you're in the process of finding out who you are.'

Megan knew her mother made sense but at the same time it was as though she was desperate to convince her that she really *was* in love with Lochie. That this wasn't just an infatuation or misplaced gratitude. That the frightening natural attraction that existed between them wasn't just because they'd both had bad relationships in the past.

'And doesn't he have a daughter?'

'Heather? Yes but that's a non-issue. She is wonderful.'

'You've spent time with her?'

'Every day after school she comes to the hospital and she needs a quiet place to do her homework so I said she could use my office.' Megan smiled as she remembered some of the conversations they'd shared. 'She's just so alive and vibrant and open. It's how Lochie is too and then there are moments when he's completely guarded and closed off. I want to be with him, to talk to him, to get him to open up to me. I want to help him.'

'That's because you're an amazing person, Megsy.'

She smiled. 'You only say that because you're my mum.'

'And I'll also say again that you need to guard your heart.'

'I know. Didn't I say I was confused?'

'You did, darling.'

Megan was silent for a moment, her thoughts working almost faster than the speed of light. 'I guess the real question I need to ask myself isn't whether or not I'm in love with Loughlin but whether I think I'll lose myself in him. That's what happened with Calvin, Mum. I lost myself in his life. I did everything for him. *Lived* my life just for him, and when he didn't want me, I felt as though my life meant nothing. I don't want to do that again. Even if I love Loughlin, I can't lose myself, my identity again. I just can't.' She looked out into the darkness. 'What am I supposed to do?'

'So you've been offered three different jobs?'

Loughlin overheard Nicole ask Megan as he walked onto

the ward. He slowed his pace a little, neither woman having seen him yet.

'Head of Unit at the Royal Melbourne and consultant positions at Brisbane and Perth hospitals.' Megan didn't sound too happy about any of them and Loughlin frowned. Why not? All three sounded to be quite viable options. 'And Jasper called last night to say a colleague of his in England has a job I might be perfect for.'

'England? You'd leave the country?' Nicole was clearly surprised.

'Why not? People have worked overseas before, Nicole.' Megan signed her name to the case notes she'd been writing and looked at her colleague.

'So which one are you going to choose?'

'I have no idea.' To say she'd been stunned by the responses to her job enquiries was an understatement. So many places to choose from, so many decisions to think on, and yet all she could think about was Loughlin and how the thought of leaving him would tear a rift in her heart. He was such an incredible man and one who'd moved halfway around the world to try something new. It was clear to everyone he met that he loved his job, that he loved helping people, fixing them when they were broken.

Well, he'd helped to fix her. Just by telling her how beautiful she was, just by kissing her the way he had, just seeing the mounting desire for her in his eyes...Megan's self-confidence had soared. Now, although it would be painful to leave him, she knew she could do it. That she would survive. She might not be completely happy without him but she was strong enough to cope. Until she'd met him, she never would have realised this about herself.

'You'd leave Loughlin?' Nicole was very surprised.

'Yes. Why did you say that? He's just another colleague.'

Nicole snorted as though she didn't believe her in the slightest. '*Right*. As if. I've seen the way the two of you look at each other.'

'What? How? How do we look at each other?'

'Like you've just seen the newest endoscope and then discovered it's selling for half-price.'

Megan stared at the CNC for a split second before bursting out laughing. 'Oh, Nicole. You are funny.'

'It's true. If I thought I had any chance with Lochie, I'd take it, but he only has eyes for you, Megan. Oh, he may charm every woman in the town but it's clearly you he's interested in.'

Megan had no idea what to say to that. Her mind, which usually worked too fast for her to keep up, was stunned at Nicole's words. She knew the whole town had been talking but she hadn't realised the talk had gone *that* far.

She heard footsteps in the corridor and turned to see the man in question walking towards them.

'Oh, hi, Lochie,' she said, her tone sounding over-bright even to her own ears.

'Hello, hello. How are things here? Patients all behaving themselves?' He smiled over-brightly at Nicole and herself.

Nicole looked from one to the other and shook her head. 'You two are insane.' At that, she headed off, leaving them alone.

'What was that about?' Megan wondered out loud.

'Apparently, we're insane. Listen, have you seen Heather?'

'No. Have you checked my—?'

'Office? Aye. She's not there.'

'It's not as though the hospital is big enough for her to get lost in so she can't be far. Would you like me to check the toilets for you?'

'If you wouldn't mind.'

'Sure.' Megan was glad to get away from the confined space of the nurses' station, especially after what Nicole had been saying. She checked the restroom but Heather wasn't in there so she decided to check her office, pleased when she found the pre-teen in there, packing up her homework. 'Hi. Your dad's looking for you.'

'OK. Thanks.' Heather smiled. 'You look really nice today, Megsy. That pink top really suits ye.'

'Uh…thanks.'

'It would look good on me, too. Think maybe I could borrow it some time?'

Megan's eyes widened at the request. 'Well…I don't see why not.'

'Ye seem surprised.'

'I've just never had anyone want to borrow my clothes before.'

'That's right. You don't have a sister. I keep forgetting. I'm used to borrowing clothes and lending mine out. I have five girl cousins as well as my aunties and we used to always share.'

'You must miss them.'

She shrugged. 'I do but they'll visit and we'll visit and it's totally the bomb being in another country.'

'You like it, then?' She hadn't been sure how the young girl would cope but Heather seemed to be quite an adaptable person, just like her dad.

'Och, aye. Especially my new school.'

'All settled in?'

'Aye.' Heather hesitated for a split second, as though she wanted to say something but was deciding whether or not she should. Even Megan could see she was about to burst so she waited patiently. 'And there's this gorgeous boy I like.'

'Boy?' Megan blinked in astonishment. 'You're only twelve,' she protested.

'And? What age did you have your first boyfriend?' Heather's lilting question had stumped Megan for a few seconds as she tried to think back.

'Not until I was at university.'

'You're joking! No wonder you went pale when I told you about sweet David in my algebra class.'

Not wanting to confess to Heather that she'd only had three boyfriends during her entire thirty-eight years—Calvin being the last—she steered the conversation away from herself. 'Have you spoken to your father about this David boy?'

'Da'?' Heather had looked at her as though she'd grown an extra head. 'No way. He'd more than likely pass out or, worse, embarrass me by becoming all protective and the like. Nay. I'm not tellin' me da'.'

Megan was unsure how to take this news. Obviously Heather felt comfortable confiding in her because she was a woman and as her aunts and cousins weren't around, it appeared she was the next best choice. In a way she was flattered to receive such a confidence but she was unsure what to do about it. 'So…uh…what does this David look like?'

At that, Heather's eyes sparkled, her face radiated pure girlish happiness. 'Nice. Really nice. He has blond hair, blue eyes and he's on the rugby team and hilariously funny. He likes my accent.'

'He likes you back?' Oh, this was getting dangerous.

'I think he does.'

'But you're only twelve!' she repeated. Megan felt so out of her depth it wasn't funny. What was she supposed to do? Tell Loughlin and break Heather's confidence? Encourage Heather to tell her father? Or just let this go and hope that the schoolgirl crush was nothing more than that…a schoolgirl crush?

'There you are.' Loughlin appeared in the doorway and looked from one female to the other.

'Found her,' Megan offered, pointing to Heather.

'I can see that.' Loughlin's expression radiated tiredness. Megan's heart yearned for him and she wanted to touch him, to run her fingers through his hair, to be held by his firm strong arms. She looked away, knowing she couldn't do any of that. 'Right, hen,' he said to Heather. 'We need to get going.' He held out the car keys to his daughter. 'You go get settled. I just need to speak to Megan for a moment.'

Megan's heart started to flutter at this announcement and nervous tension prickled its way along her spine. Anxiety settled into her chest but she did some deep breathing to control it.

'Right ye are, Da'.' Heather said goodbye to Megan and headed out. Loughlin closed the door and turned to look at the woman who was plaguing his thoughts, his dreams, his every waking moment.

'Something wrong?' she asked when he didn't immediately talk.

'You sound a little breathless.'

'I'm fine.'

'You have anxiety, don't you.' It was a statement. 'You get chest pains and you use your breathing to control them.'

'So?' Megan was a little puzzled. 'You wanted to talk to me about my anxiety?'

'No. I mean yes. I didn't know you *had* anxiety.'

'You didn't need to know.'

'Of course I did. I work with you. I'm in Theatre with you. What if you had suffered from such terrible pains that you'd collapsed? I would have needed to know why.'

'As that hasn't happened, I think this discussion is over.'

'How bad are they, Megan?'

'Not bad at all.'

'Yet you're having them now?'

'If I am, it's no one's business but my own.' Megan bristled at his tone, at his high-handedness.

'Are you on medication for the pains?'

'No.'

'Have you seen a specialist? Had one of your chums check you over?'

'No.'

'Then you're a fool.'

'Apparently, but I am also a qualified surgeon who is more than capable of handling her own problems.'

'As is evident.'

'What is that supposed to mean?' Why was he intent on attacking her all of a sudden?

Loughlin unhooked his stethoscope from around his neck and

put it in his ears. 'I'm going to listen to your chest and give you a diagnosis right now.'

'You are not.' She backed away from him. 'Loughlin McCloud, you are way out of line.'

'Out of line?' He stared at her. 'The woman I can't stop thinking about, the woman who's been driving me crazy for weeks now, is having chest pains and is refusing to do anything about it.'

Megan worked hard at focusing on the last part of his sentence because the first part only made her want to throw herself into his arms even more than before. It was strange how she could be so cross with him yet at the same time be desperate for him to kiss her.

'I *am* doing something about it.'

'What?' He advanced a few steps towards her.

'I'm monitoring and controlling it. It's nowhere near as bad as it used to be. Kiama has been good for me in that respect but it's emotional anxiety, Loughlin, and right now *you're* the one who's making it worse so back off!'

'Why?' he pushed. He knew he was being irrational, knew he was causing her to say things she probably wasn't ready to say, to say things she probably *shouldn't* say because it would only make the heartache he experienced far worse. 'Why do I make it worse? Tell me, Megan.' He took another step towards her, literally backing her into a corner.

'Because I can't stop thinking about you either. Lochie, this isn't going to get us anywhere. You know it. I know it. We're attracted to each other but it can never work.' The words tumbled out of her mouth. If he came any closer, she wasn't sure she was going to be able to control her urge to press her mouth to his. By the way he was looking at her, his gaze flicking between her lips and her eyes, his expression letting her know he'd be more than contented to devour her right here, right now, it was paramount they put distance between them.

'So you're saying we need to stop it?' He was within a half a metre of her and Megan put up her hands to keep him away.

'Yes.'

'And you're going to do that by moving away? By accepting another job?'

'Yes. I told you the first day we met that I didn't think I'd be staying in Kiama and now I'm positive that I need to leave.'

'Even though the people here consider you one of their own? Even though you're as much a part of this community as anyone else? You may not have realised it, Megan, but you are. You fit here. You belong here.'

'No, I don't. I don't belong anywhere.'

She was wrong about that. 'You fit perfectly in my arms,' he murmured, pulling his stethoscope off and tossing it carefully onto her desk. 'Let me show you.'

'No.' His words had made her heart beat triple time, her breathing shallow and her desire for him so hot and heavy she was finding it difficult to concentrate.

'You need to sound more convincing than that, Megsy.' He was so close now, their breaths mingled, fusing together. 'I cannae stop thinking about you. I cannae stop wanting you, needing you. I know it's wrong but it feels so right.' His whispered words pierced her heart, her chest pains subsiding within an instant as she began to relax, began to realise she wanted him to kiss her as much as he wanted to kiss her.

Without touching her, he leaned forward and brushed his lips across her own. Megan quivered with mounting anticipation. It was on the tip of her tongue to tell him she loved him, that she wanted to make this work, that she wanted to be with him for ever, but she couldn't. What if it didn't work? What if things went wrong? What if she lost her identity again?

'Megsy,' he breathed, and came closer. Still not touching her, except for his lips on hers, he deepened the kiss. It was as though there was an invisible forcefield around her that he couldn't break through, except for her lips. He focused on the taste, the touch of them against his, and wondered if anything else in his life would ever be this perfect.

The way she responded was something else he wasn't sure he'd be able to give up. So wholeheartedly, so passionately, so unreservedly. If he were a man about to go to the gallows, this would be his last request…to kiss Megan Edwards because the way she made him feel would last an eternity. And it might need to.

Loughlin knew there was too much pain in their pasts for them to wade through. Although he loved Megan, he couldn't bring himself to tell her. To confess such feelings only made him vulnerable and he'd vowed never to put himself in that position again. What if it didn't work? What if things went wrong? What if he failed at marriage yet again?

The kiss was slow yet thorough, her hands firmly by her sides, knowing if she gave in to those urges she was now desperately fighting she might never let him go. And she had to let him go. She knew it. He knew it. This attraction couldn't last and if she allowed herself to throw caution to the wind, she'd wind up even more hurt than before because Loughlin meant far more to her than any other man ever had.

With one last touch, one last moment of drinking her in, one last opportunity to memorise the way her lips felt on his, he pulled away. Their breathing was uneven and he knew she was just as affected by him as he was by her. At least this time it wasn't one-sided. It wasn't as it had been with Bonnie and he knew that what he felt for Megan was far more intense than what he'd experienced with his ex-wife. That was the reason why he was now desperate to stay away from the woman before him.

Neither of them spoke, both of them taking their time to open their eyes and gaze at each other. 'You really are beautiful.' The words were whispered from his lips before he realised he was speaking out loud.

'So are you.'

Loughlin shook his head sadly. 'But it can't work.'

'No.'

'You're going to leave?'

'Yes.'

'Where to?'

'I'm not sure.'

'England?' He watched her eyes widen for a moment as though she was trying to figure out how he knew but she relaxed again, knowing he'd either overheard her or heard it from someone else. Small community. Small hospital. Everyone knew everything.

'Perhaps.' She shrugged.

'Let me know what you decide. I have some good friends there and, of course, my family is not so far away. They'll look after you. Make sure you feel welcome and that way you won't have to feel so lonely.' There was immense sadness in his voice as he spoke. He looked at her lips again and for a split second she thought he might kiss her again but, instead, he took a big step backwards, putting much-needed distance between them.

'Goodbye, Megan.'

They both knew she wasn't leaving the hospital for at least another month but his goodbye had nothing at all to do with that. Whatever had been between them was now firmly decided to be nothing more than what it had been. They'd both agreed on that. It was done. It was over.

'Goodbye, Loughlin.' As she watched him walk to the door, her heart was pierced with the most amazing pain and she instinctively knew it wasn't anxiety…it was her heart breaking.

CHAPTER TEN

MEGAN looked at the mound of papers before her and shook her head. Plans for her flights to England in just over five weeks' time, accommodation, hospital appointments. Red tape in all its glory. Right now, she wanted none of it. She'd always known she would leave Kiama. It had never been a permanent move, a permanent option. So why was she feeling so sick at the thought of going?

Loughlin had been right when he'd said she'd become a part of this community. She knew almost everyone in town, knew her staff well. She was well liked and people respected her. Even though she'd tried to hold herself apart, to remain aloof—prickly, as Loughlin had termed it—it hadn't succeeded. She liked being here.

Or was it because of Loughlin that she liked being in Kiama? She loved him, more so than when he'd said goodbye to her last week. Since then they'd remained polite and aloof, treating each other as nothing more than colleagues. Other people had commented on it and Nicole had even complained that Loughlin wasn't his usual jovial self any more. Megan had agreed and realised that it was sad not to see him being happy.

But it was worth it. The heartache, the pain, it would all be worth it and it would all be temporary. Leaving Kiama was the grown-up thing to do. Putting distance between herself and

Loughlin was the responsible, self-preserving thing to do and that was why she was doing it. She had to keep sight of that.

Heather, on the other hand, hadn't been at all impressed to find Megan was planning to leave. 'Who am I supposed to confide in now?' she asked angrily.

'There are plenty of other nice people for you to talk to.' Megan had remained calm.

'But I like you. So does my da'. I know you both really like each other so it's totally ridiculous when you go on about leaving.'

'My job here is coming to an end, Heather. I need to work and there is work for me in England.' Her tone had held a hint of finality and when the teenager had opened her mouth to argue further, Megan had said firmly, 'Leave it now.'

Feeling tears beginning to prickle as she remembered the distraught look on Heather's face, Megan closed her eyes, trying to hold them at bay. She needed to focus on work. Work would help her. It would get her through. She opened her eyes and sat up straighter, looking at the work before her. After a minute she realised it was pointless. Her head was starting to pound with the beginning of a headache and her breathing was becoming tight once again.

When she heard footsteps outside, her heart quickened, her hands clenching together. A second later a loud knock at her door made her jump.

'Megsy?'

'Heather?' Megan quickly crossed to the door to find the girl, dressed in her pyjamas and slippers, hair all tousled from sleep, eyes wide with alarm, breathing laboured. 'What's wrong?' Megan was instantly on her guard as she pulled on her coat, rushing to the nearby cupboard where she kept her medical kit before collecting her house keys. 'Is it your dad? Is he all right? What's going on? Are you OK?'

'Da's fine,' she panted, rubbing her side where she'd obviously got a stitch from running. 'Come on. You need your car keys.'

'What's happened? Where are we going?'

Heather turned and walked towards where Megan's new car was parked, waiting for her to unlock it with the remote. Megan watched as the girl's breathing slowly returned to normal.

'Heather, are *you* all right?'

'I'm fine.' She waved Megan's words away with the same mannerism as her father. 'Let's get going. Da' should be there by now.'

'Where?' Megan started the engine and switched on the headlights.

'A man came knocking at our door about ten minutes ago. He was totally freaking out and said his wife was in labour and that he'd hit a tree and he couldn't get her to the hospital and she was really starting to push and everything.' Heather sort of shrugged as they drove towards the main road.

'Where are they? Do you know? Did your dad tell you?'

'Da' just grabbed his bag and told me to go and get you. He said he'd call the hospital and alert them but that he needed you.' Heather grinned widely at Megan. 'See? My da' needs you. Isn't that a good thing?'

Megan glanced quickly over at the girl. 'I don't think that was what he meant, Heather, and now is certainly not the time to be discussing it.'

'But you like my da', yeah?'

Megan really didn't want to get into a discussion about this so thought it best to simply answer the question and get on with it. 'Of course I like him. We're friends.'

'*More* than friends. You like him the way I like David. I can see it in your eyes when you look at him.'

'Heather.' There was a warning tone in Megan's voice but Heather simply laughed.

'You sound like Auntie Georgie. She always says I'm far too inquisitive for my own good. Don't worry, I'll leave you alone.' Heather giggled then sobered. 'After all, what we're doing out here is serious.'

'Exactly.' Megan swung the car onto the main road. 'Where am I supposed to be going?'

'Da' said to head for the main road and—there…' Heather pointed to where there was a bright light coming from the head-lights of her father's car. Megan brought the car to a skidding halt and quickly reversed to shine the headlights of her own car so they provided maximum illumination.

'Nice piece of driving,' Loughlin commented as she walked towards him, medical bag in hand. Megan worked hard on con-trolling the way his nearness made her feel. This wasn't the time. Or the place.

'Thanks. How's the labour progressing?' She walked up to the car and noted the crumpled bonnet against the tree. Whilst the car wasn't drivable, the interior of the car hadn't been as affected. The woman was thankfully in the rear of the car, stretched out along the back seat, her legs up as she lay back and panted, often grunting in discomfort.

'She's dilated.' Loughlin couldn't get over how incredible Megan looked and seeing her away from the four walls of the hospital only made it more difficult for him to control his thoughts.

'Fully?' Megan was surprised.

'Aye.'

'And you've called the ambulance?'

'Aye. Take a look at Derek. I'll keep an eye on Eva.' Loughlin pointed to where the expectant father was sitting on the ground near a rear wheel of the car. He looked worn out and quite dejected.

'Hi, there.' She walked towards him. 'I'm Megan.'

'Derek.' His tone was flat and she put her medical bag down and opened it.

'How are you feeling? Anything hurting?'

'No.' He shook his head but still looked off into nothingness. 'I can't believe I crashed. I didn't mean to crash. I just wanted to get her to the hospital as quickly as I could and she was panting and in so much pain in the back and I turned to look at her and then when I looked back, the tree was…' He stopped, his voice rising, and Megan immediately shushed him.

'Eva's doing fine. The ambulance is on its way and you chose the right house to go to for help. Every thing's going to be fine, Derek. Lochie and I are used to this sort of thing.' She pulled out her medical torch and checked his pupils, pleased to see they were both equal and reacting to light.

'What? People crashing their cars into trees while trying to get their wife to hospital so she can give birth?'

Megan's lips twitched. 'Well, not that *exact* scenario but we're used to emergencies.'

'I just didn't see the tree.' Derek's tone was at least less hysterical than it had been before.

'I know. Now, can you tell me where you hurt?' She placed her hands at the back of his neck to check for a whiplash injury. 'Did the seat belt cut into you? Did you hit your head?'

'The air-bags went off and stunned me but— Ow.' He groaned as she touched his neck and trapezius.

'I think I'd like to get a neck brace on you at least. Better to be safe than sorry. Apart from the odd scratch and bruise, I think you'll be fine.' She'd just finished putting a collar around his neck when Loughlin called her over. Heather was now around the other side of the car, having climbed in next to Eva. She was dabbing the woman's forehead with a handkerchief and talking quietly to her.

'What's going on?' Megan asked.

'Baby's breech.' Loughlin said quietly. 'She's just had a contraction and I had a look for the head but I'm not seeing it.'

Megan pulled on a pair of gloves and called out to Eva. 'Keep breathing nice and easy, Eva. I'm just going to take a look.' Megan bent down, not even needing to ask Loughlin to angle his torch because he was already doing it.

'Definitely breech,' she confirmed. 'Well, if we can angle Eva so we have better access, that might help.' She looked over at Eva. 'Is this your first child?'

'Yes.' Eva panted through the pain. 'Derek? Where's Derek?'

'I'll get him sorted,' Loughlin said. 'Dads need to be on duty at this special time in their lives or they'll regret it for ever.'

Megan listened to his words, hearing the change in his tone, the resonance in his meaning, and wondered if he'd been present for Heather's unexpectedly early birth. There was simply so much she didn't know about this man, this man she loved. She *wanted* to know everything about him but knew she'd sound presumptuous if she started asking questions, especially as they'd already said goodbye.

Sure enough, Loughlin had Derek taking over from Heather, supporting his wife and being there to kiss her forehead and murmur soothing words. 'He feels as though he's failed her,' Loughlin said quietly when he came to stand next to Megan.

'How so?'

'By crashing the car? By leaving her while he went to get help?'

'Mobile phone had no reception?'

'Correct.'

'Heather said you've called this in?'

'I called it from on top of the hill before the reception went bad.'

'Good. Hopefully, we can try and keep things moving along until the ambulance turns up. First babies usually take longer to deliver and I have to confess I'd be far more comfortable doing this delivery in the hos—' Her words were cut short as Eva had another contraction and this one was a beauty. She hollered and screamed her way through the pain. Megan focused on what was happening.

'It's bad enough trying to push out the baby's head,' Loughlin remarked quietly once the contraction had eased.

'And you'd know?' Megan raised an eyebrow at him and he grinned at her. Heather was standing near them, holding the torch, interestedly watching the exchange between the adults. She didn't appear at all squeamish about the impending birth.

'I'll have you know that I've assisted in the delivery of two of my nephews and one of my nieces. Heather was present at the last birth and that's when she told me she was going to follow in my footsteps and be a doctor.'

'I want to deliver babies. It's totally awesome,' Heather piped up.

'Well, you'll be getting an education tonight,' Megan replied. She pulled out her stethoscope and listened for the baby's heartbeat. Loughlin checked on Eva and both doctors were pleased with the way things were progressing.

When the next contraction came, it was stronger than the last and Eva needed to keep on pushing as the baby's buttocks started really showing.

'The perineum is too tight,' Loughlin commented to Megan.

'Agreed. Heather, I need you to get some things out of my medical kit for me.' Megan told the girl what she wanted and soon Heather had located the injection of local anaesthetic and handed it to Megan.

'You're quite adept. As good as your father.'

'I like this.' Heather shrugged as though she assisted with surgery every day. When the local anaesthetic had taken effect, and after another contraction, Megan took the sterilised surgical scissors from the packet Heather held open to her and then performed an episiotomy. Once that was done, the labour seemed to progress quite quickly.

'Ambulance is here,' Heather announced, after both the feet had been delivered and Loughlin was holding carefully onto the baby's hips, being careful not to hold the baby by the abdomen or flanks to avoid causing kidney or liver damage.

When the paramedics came up, Megan gave them explicit instructions. 'Have the oxytocin ready, ten units intramuscular. I'll need clamps and scissors. Be ready with the suction.'

Gav, Kiama's police officer, turned up as well and as Loughlin and Megan assisted with the delivery of the baby's arms, one at a time, Gav started taking control of the emergency situation. By the time the baby boy was delivered, Eva was utterly exhausted. She wasn't all that interested in holding or seeing the baby straight away and Megan hoped she didn't reject the baby because of the abnormal circumstances of his birth.

Derek, however, was as chuffed as you would imagine a new father could be. 'We're going to call him David Nicholas.'

'Lovely,' Megan replied.

'David's a great name,' Heather piped up, with a wink at Megan.

'Good, strong names,' Loughlin added, shaking the man's hand. His car was a wreck, his wife was exhausted but he was a proud father and nothing was going to dampen this moment for him, not even the light rain that was starting to fall. Megan delivered the placenta while Lochie, with Heather's help, performed observations on the baby—pleased with the results. Soon, they were able to get Eva ready for transfer into the ambulance.

Megan climbed in to the back of the emergency vehicle to give Eva a quick check. 'You're doing very well.'

'I'm tired.' She turned her head away.

'I know. Did you want to see little David Nicholas?'

'Nicholas David,' she contradicted. 'If he tries to call my son David, after his father rather than Nicholas after my father, he's got another think coming.'

Megan soothed Eva and decided it was best to get the new little family to the hospital sooner rather than later. 'I'll follow the ambulance in my car and see you at the hospital.'

'Whatever.' Eva resolutely closed her eyes and Megan climbed from the vehicle.

As they stood there, Loughlin, Megan and Heather watching the ambulance pull away, Megan shook her head.

'What?' Loughlin asked. Megan turned to look at him and saw that he had his arm around Heather's shoulders, holding his daughter close.

'Nothing.'

'Ah, it's not nothing, Megan Iris. I can read your thoughts.'

'Is that so?' She looked at him, pleased to see that for this moment at least he was his old self. Perhaps they hadn't finished saying goodbye after all?

'Aye.'

'Then what am I thinking?'

'You're trying to figure out how a woman cannae want to see her child. Can possibly not care what happens to him. Of course, rationally, you tell yourself that it's just because she's been through one heck of an ordeal and is completely exhausted—both of which are true. You're sure that later on she'll want to hold her baby, to nurse him, to bond with him.'

'She will. A lot of mothers are just too exhausted.' Megan started packing up her medical kit, keeping out of Gav's way as he spoke to the tow-truck driver.

'Not all mothers bond with their babies.' Loughlin's words were spoken quietly and Megan instantly straightened, looking at him. Loughlin dropped a kiss to Heather's head, the girl leaning into him.

Megan wished she had a camera to capture the moment, the look of love, trust and protectiveness that passed from Loughlin to his daughter. He'd told her how Heather's mother hadn't been interested in the girl and, after meeting Heather and spending time with her, Megan had come to the conclusion that Loughlin's ex-wife had a few screws loose.

'Her loss.' The words were out of her mouth before she realised it and she soon found two pairs of identical brown eyes turned her way. 'Heather—you're amazing.' Megan's words were sincere and straight from the heart. 'If your mother doesn't want to know you, she is missing out—big time—on someone who is not only a brilliant young woman but is going to reach for the stars and impress us all as she continues to grow.' Tears started to gather in Megan's eyes and she was stunned that she could feel so vehement about her love for this twelve-year-old.

Heather left her father's side and ran to Megan, hugging her close. 'That was really nice. What you said.'

Megan looked at the girl, who was almost her height. 'It's all true.' And in that moment, as she held Heather close, Megan felt the twinges of maternal instinct kick in. It was something she'd denied herself for so long, had thought she'd never get to experience, and here she was, absolutely crazy about Loughlin's daughter. Was it easy to love the child because she loved the father? Or was it simply that both McClouds had worked their way into her heart, letting her see there was far more to life than working and trying to cope with the past?

'We'd better get to the hospital.' Loughlin was the one to break the moment but he didn't say anything else. Even as he bundled Heather back into his ute, he didn't speak much at all.

'Wouldn't it be easier for all of us to go in one car?' Heather asked, but the only answer she received was a shake of her father's head.

Loughlin checked his rear-view mirror and saw Megan talking briefly with Gav, who would wait around for the tow-truck driver to leave. His heart lurched at the sight of Megan as he watched the smooth way she moved, the way she put a hand on Gav's shoulder. He could see her lips moving and even though he couldn't hear her, he knew she was thanking the police officer. She was quite a woman and he couldn't believe *she* didn't see that. He was so angry at the jerk who had left her at the altar because not only had he humiliated her, he'd stripped her of all her self-confidence. He wanted to shake her sometimes, to tell her she was the most vibrant, exciting and intoxicating woman he'd ever met.

His heart swelled with love for her and the need for them to be together intensified…but he knew that couldn't be.

Forcing himself to look away from Megan, he returned his focus to the road before him, on this dark and not so stormy night. He couldn't think about the way Megan had embraced Heather and the words she'd spoken. He needed to concentrate on getting to the hospital safely but flashes of Megan holding Heather, the way she'd looked at the girl with such maternal love, had definitely rocked him to his core.

It was what he'd been wanting his ex-wife to do for so long…well, for the past twelve years, but every time Bonnie had come back into his and Heather's life, she'd left them broken up and dejected. He'd watched as Heather had become quite attached to Megan over the past weeks, the two of them instantly bonding, and where he'd been happy to see his daughter settling in, he'd been wary of her getting too close to Megan.

He loved Megan. He'd admitted as much to himself. It was obvious his daughter loved Megan too but he hadn't expected Megan—the woman who'd said she was too prickly to let people into her life—to love his daughter back. It just showed him how much she'd changed since they'd first met. She didn't appear to be looking backwards all the time, trying to reconcile her past. Instead, he hoped her eyes were steadfastly on the future…whatever it might bring.

At the hospital, he was able to concentrate much better, ensuring baby Nicholas David or David Nicholas was improving rapidly. By the time Megan arrived, he'd organised for the new family to have a quiet room of their own, Derek not wanting to let his new son out of his sight.

'How's Eva?' Megan made sure she didn't stand too close to Loughlin as she asked the question. They were in the ward where Nicole, the CNC, was enjoying having a newborn to fuss over.

'Exhibiting signs of emotional distress and early onset of postnatal depression. I've given her a sedative to help her sleep.'

'Good.' Megan read the chart and the observations that had been performed. Silence reigned between them.

'Er…did Gav get everything sorted out?'

Megan's smile was immediate. 'Have you ever known Gav *not* to get things sorted out?'

'True.' He watched her, knowing she was giving the chart before her far more attention than it deserved.

'Uh…Megan?'

'Yes?'

'Thanks.' He shifted a little and made sure he was looking her directly into her eyes as he spoke. 'Thanks for saying what you did about Heather.'

'It's all true, Lochie. She's amazing. You've done a brilliant job in raising her. You should be immensely proud.'

'Aye. I am. No doubt about that.'

'Where is Heather, by the way?'

'In your office, I think. It's her favourite place in the hospital.' Megan's smile was immediate. 'So she's told me.'

'You've become quite close.'

Megan nodded. 'I love her, Loughlin. I'm sorry if that makes you feel uncomfortable or concerned or whatever, but she's touched a part of me deep inside.' Megan put the chart down and laced her fingers together. 'She reminds me of me. When I was twelve I had such drive, such determination to become a doctor. My teachers were astounded at my comprehension levels and natural ability to do my work so easily that at Heather's age I had an IQ test, discovered I was in the "genius" category and haven't looked back since.'

'Is that so?' Loughlin wasn't all that surprised. He'd figured out quite quickly that Megan was highly intelligent but he'd had no idea she'd been branded with the genius label. 'That must have raised the bar a little. Made life a wee bit more difficult.'

Megan shrugged. 'Workwise, things were easy. I breezed through school.'

'I didn't mean at an academic level. I mean, with that sort of intellect, people expect more from you.' He studied her closely, as though really seeing her for the first time. 'Expect you to grow up faster. Be more mature than you are simply because you have a higher level of comprehension.'

Megan thought about it. 'I guess. Yes.' She was feeling quite unnerved with what he was saying and realised she should shift the conversation away from herself. 'And that's why I think it's been so easy for me to accept Heather. She's incredibly smart, Lochie.'

'I ken that.'

'But at the same time she's a normal twelve-year-old.'

'And you envy that a wee bit, eh? No doubt you were thrust out of your normal world into an adult world and expected to behave like one.' He wanted to touch her, to caress her cheek, to hold her close. He kept his hands firmly at his sides. 'You didn't have time to find out who you really were—apart from being a smart girl.'

Tears had sprung to Megan's eyes at his soft, heartfelt words. It was as though while he was speaking she was coming to realise the full truth of his words. She'd never been a normal teenager. She'd been the freaky genius girl who her peers had only spoken to if they'd wanted help with their homework. It was a mould she'd allowed herself to be put into because in a way it had given her a level of acceptance amongst her peers, an identity of sorts. She'd closed herself off back then and she'd allowed other people—her teachers, her university lecturers, her hospital superiors—to keep her in the same mould.

'I'd forgotten how perceptive you are.' She smiled through the tears, trying to get control.

'Och, Megsy.' Loughlin couldn't stand it any longer and went to reach for her, needing to hold her close to him. She instantly backed away and swiped a hand across her eyes. He dropped his hand. 'I didn't mean to make you cry.'

'I need to go.' She fished her car keys from her pocket and pulled a tissue from the box on the nurses' desk.

Loughlin stepped forward and took her hand in his. 'You drive carefully, you hear?'

She looked down at their hands, at the way they were intertwined, and for a second she couldn't tell which were her fingers and which were his. His warmth instantly seeped into her, igniting the fire deep within and making her heart pound with love.

She nodded and disengaged herself from the touch. 'I will.'
She cleared her throat. 'Are you OK to finish up here?'

'Aye.'

She turned and headed towards her office, needing to check
on Heather before she left. The girl was sitting in Megan's chair,
half leaning over the desk as she dozed.

'Hey,' she whispered, and brushed Heather's hair from her eyes.

'Megsy? Is it time to go?'

'Your dad needs to stay for a bit longer.'

'You're heading home?'

'Yes.'

'I'm coming with you,' she declared. 'Is my da' on the ward?'

'Yes.' Megan watched as Heather picked up the phone,
dialled the extension number, spoke to her father and then
replaced the receiver.

'All done. I'm sleeping at your place tonight.' She stood and
slipped her arm around Megan. 'Let's go. I'm so tired.'

And just like that Megan found herself driving them back to her
place. It wasn't that she minded having Heather with her. Quite the
opposite—she loved it—but it simply meant that she'd more than
likely need to see Loughlin earlier than usual the next morning.

What would happen when they saw each other? Would he
come to her place or would it be easier for her to walk Heather
the distance between their two houses? Would he expect to eat
breakfast with her? Would he look at her over the top of his coffee-
cup the way he'd looked at her before, his eyes rich with repressed
desire? Would he try to touch her again? Hold her? Kiss her?

Her heart was racing with the possibilities, her mind trying
to play through every scenario to try and come up with one that
worked best to her advantage and also kept her heart firm and
secure. She looked over at Heather, who was snoozing in the passenger seat.

'Do you like my da'?' That was the question Heather had
asked earlier on that night and Megan had wanted to scream it

from the rooftops that she didn't just *like* him, she *loved* him. In one breath she wanted the whole world to know and in the next she wanted to lock her heart up for ever, to ensure it never got hurt again.

Falling in love with Loughlin McCloud had brought her a whole new set of problems and she honestly had no idea how to deal with them. She wished she didn't have a brain that needed to process everything, that needed to not only think in a logical and rational way but to find the answers that made the most sense—even if it meant denying herself the happiness she'd always craved.

Twenty minutes later, Heather was wrapped up all snuggly and warm in Megan's spare room and she'd just made herself a cup of soothing herbal tea, needing *something* to help relax her mind and body. Tonight's emergency had nothing to do with the way she felt. She was used to the stress that went with her job. No, the reason she needed to relax was quite simply because of the man who was seductive, sexy and Scottish.

She had to figure out what to do to save not only her sanity but her heart as well. She was in love with a man she saw every day. She melted into a mess of hormones whenever he was near. She felt as though her heart would stop at the slightest hint of the electrified tension that existed between them.

How on earth was she supposed to survive?

The following morning, Megan was doing her best to avoid seeing Loughlin after Heather's impromptu sleepover. What she hadn't been able to avoid were the girl's questions.

'Why don't you come and have breakfast with us? Da' would love it.'

Megan had quickly declined. 'I don't think so, Heather.'

'Why not? Da' won't mind. Not at all. You know he likes you,' she teased in a sing-song way that had Megan's cheeks tingeing with colour.

'That's beside the point. Actually, I have a lot to get done this morning.' Megan tidied her already tidy kitchen, avoiding looking directly at Heather.

'You told me last night that you like my da'.'

'And I do. Everyone likes your father. He's a very personable man.' She shrugged and dried her hands on the tea-towel.

'But you *like*-like him. I can tell. He like-likes you back. The *real* way.' The girl's grin was wide and she waggled her eyebrows up and down for effect, making Megan smile.

'Let's not go there.'

'Why not? Why are you both too scared to be together? Honestly. I don't understand grown-ups at all. You like him. He likes you. You both want to be together. Even a blind man could see that so I don't have a clue why you're planning to leave us.'

'It's not that I'm leaving *you*, Heather, it's just that—'

She wasn't able to finish her sentence as there was a brief knock at her front door and Loughlin called out, 'Anybody home?'

'Da'?' Heather bounced from the kitchen, missing the colour draining from Megan's face.

Megan closed her eyes and tried to pull herself together, knowing he'd be with her in a few seconds. She needed to keep it light. Keep it professional and neighbourly. Nothing more. So why did all of her good intentions slip away the instant he walked into her kitchen?

'Morning, Megsy.' His voice was rich and deep and so incredibly sexy that she instantly reached out a hand to the bench beside her for support. He gave her a quick visual caress, taking in the long flowing black skirt and bright blue top, which only served to highlight her amazing eyes. He swallowed, unable to look away. Her hair was loose, silky and shiny, and he itched to touch it, to have it sift through his fingers, the scent of whatever shampoo and conditioner she used driving him to distraction as he breathed it in. Honestly, the woman was becoming far too irresistible for her own good.

'Hi.' Her lips barely moved as she formed the word.

Then neither spoke and Loughlin knew they had to seriously figure out how to deal with this attraction a lot better than they were doing at present. The kitchen seemed to shrink in size, Loughlin filling it with his presence, Heather somewhere on the outskirts but momentarily forgotten as Megan drank in her fill of him.

He was dressed in that comfortable pair of denims he liked best, a striped shirt with a thin woollen jumper over the top, the shirt tails hanging out at both front and back. His feet had been shoved into a pair of casual boat shoes and his fingers had obviously been the only source for combing his spiky hair as it was all sticking up on end. The whole ensemble had no doubt been thrown on without a care in the world as he'd rushed over to see his daughter. Yet the effect was most definitely breathtaking.

'Da'.' It was Heather who broke the moment. 'Megsy was saying she wanted to have breakfast with us.'

Loughlin raised his eyebrows at this. 'Is that so?'

'No. No. It's fine,' Megan said spluttering. 'I've got lots of things to get done today. Don't want to get held up.'

'It's breakfast, Megsy,' Loughlin pointed out, deciding on the spur of the moment that perhaps they should. They needed another set of guidelines so they both knew how to behave when they ran into each other in circumstances such as these. At least, that was what he was telling himself when he knew the real reason he wanted to prolong this contact, the real reason why he'd jogged all the way to her place that morning, why he wanted to stand there gazing into her eyes, was because he loved her so completely that he wanted to be with her.

'Breakfast is the most important meal of the day, remember?' he continued, needing to persuade her. 'Now, as a medical practitioner and also as a pillar of this community, I think it's only right that you follow the prescription you would no doubt give to all of your patients, to start the day right.'

Why was it that when he spoke like that, when his lilting

words were already creating havoc with her all her senses, he had to look at her lips? It was as though he was saying that kissing her lips would be the better way to start every day, and she knew her body was no doubt giving him the answer that he was correct.

Before she'd kissed Lochie, she'd only been able to wonder and speculate, which had been fine for her. Dreaming about what it would be like to be held in his arms, to have him hold her body close, to feel that sweet pressure, that sensual taste that was totally *him*…she'd been content to simply dream.

But then he had kissed her. He had held her close. He had shown her what she was missing and she had responded by loving him. Oh, how she desperately wanted him to kiss her now. Couldn't he see that? Couldn't he feel it? Didn't he want it too?

'Er…Heather.' Without taking his eyes off Megan, he spoke to his daughter. 'Why don't you go and call Paula and book us a table for breakfast? Megsy won't mind if you use her phone.'

'Go ahead,' Megan heard herself respond, her eyes still locked with Loughlin's, her body trembling at the need she saw reflected in the man before her.

'The three of us?' Heather asked, oblivious to the silent conversation passing between the two adults.

'Yes.' Loughlin heard Heather's squeal of excitement as she ran off to use Megan's phone to make the call but his attention was focused solely on the woman before him. 'Megsy.' His voice was soft, his gaze flicking between her eyes and her mouth, causing her breathing rate to increase. She parted her lips to allow the pent-up air to escape and Loughlin almost groaned with longing.

He'd realised last night as he'd assisted with the miracle of birth that he desperately wanted more children. He wanted a loving mother and wife to be by his side and the woman who stood before him was exactly who he'd pictured. She loved his daughter completely and that had only served to enhance his own love for her.

Earlier that morning, when he hadn't been able to sleep be-

cause his thoughts had been filled with a multitude of different
scenarios about exactly what he should do with regard to his
feelings for Megan, Loughlin had realised that if he didn't do
something he might just miss his opportunity. He knew she'd
leave. That she would go to England and get on with her life
unless he did something.

As those thoughts had entered his mind, he'd started to realise
that he wouldn't be able to see her every day. He wouldn't be
able to talk to her, to make her laugh, to see that sparkle in her
eyes when she teased him, to have her addictive scent wash over
him. To have none of that had left him feeling even more hollow
than he'd felt after his divorce.

He needed her…so he needed to take some chances. Big
chances. Big steps into the unknown. He knew he'd regret it if
he didn't and he wasn't going to live on regrets any more.

'Megsy,' he said again. 'There's something on my mind.'

'What's that?' Her words were but a breathless whisper as she
realised he'd somehow closed the distance between them,
although she hadn't been aware of him moving.

'This.'

With a gasp of delight and relief Megan found herself caught
up in his arms, his mouth pressed to hers in one swift movement.
She sighed into his arms, her lips accepting his in welcome, and
her heart conveyed all the love she held for him.

His mouth moved over hers in a slow and meticulous fashion,
much as he'd done that very first time he'd kissed her out in his
car. Back then he'd been intent on helping her to create a happy
memory but now this kiss had nothing to do with happy
memories but highly sensual ones…sensual ones she wanted to
not only keep but to follow through with.

His arms tightened, their bodies pressed as close as they
possibly could, and where she'd thought the hunger and passion
he obviously felt for her would come bursting forth, he continued to exhibit immense control yet at the same time his explo-

ration of her mouth, of her senses, of her heart, was deep and thorough. Rich and warm. Mind-blowing and exhilarating.

As he pulled back, he left her swooning, her head spinning with thoughts of him and the beauty they somehow managed to create together. Her eyes were still closed, her lips plump and gently parted, her breathing as erratic as his own. She was a vision of loveliness and he wondered what she'd do if he declared his love for her.

Would she run and hide? Would she stand her ground? Would she simply drag his head back to her own? He hoped it was the last. He opened his mouth to speak but stopped when she sighed and murmured against him, her head coming to rest on his shoulder.

'Mmm. Lochie.' Her eyes opened and he looked down into her drowsy bedroom eyes. 'I just want you to know that you can speak your mind…any…time. That's fine by me, laddie.'

He couldn't help the grin that touched his lips, or the hope that filled his heart. 'I might just do that.' He pressed a firm but sound kiss to her lips.

'I thought this wouldn't ever happen again.'

'Me, too.'

'I know we've said goodbye, that we've decided that we shouldn't pursue this thing between us, but, Loughlin…' She stopped and closed her eyes, tears starting to gather. 'I've missed you.'

'Och, Megsy, I've missed you, too.' He kissed her once again, needing to show her just how much he'd missed her, gathering her as close to him as he possibly could. This time when he pulled back and looked down into her eyes, he shook his head. 'And I'd ask you to stop looking at me like that, especially when my daughter is in the next room.'

'Looking at you?

'With those rich come-hither eyes. Between them and your soft pouty lips, it's difficult enough for me to even think.'

'That's good.'

'It is? Then let us hope that an emergency doesn't come in.'

'Let someone else deal with the emergencies.' She shook her head slowly and sighed. 'I want to stay right where I am. Right here.' She snuggled her head against his chest again and breathed in deeply, the scent that was now synonymous with him filling her senses. How could she even think of leaving? Think of moving to the other side of the world when everything that was important to her was in this house? Loughlin and Heather. She loved them both so intensely, her heart was bubbling over with the emotion.

'Is that so?' He stroked her hair.

'Aye.'

He could hear the laughter in her throat. 'Are you teasing me?'

'Aye,' she repeated, but didn't move from where she was. She probably figured he wouldn't retaliate if he was holding her close in his arms and she was right. Holding her close like this was something he'd been dreaming about on such a regular basis of late it wasn't funny.

'You already know the penalty for teasing a Scotsman and still you're willing to do it?'

'Och, aye.' Now she did pull back to look at him, a delighted smile on her face, a meaningful look in her eyes. 'And I'm looking forward to paying the price.' She rolled her r's as she spoke and winked at him. Loughlin's eyes widened with absolute pleasure.

'Megan Iris! Where's the reserved, prickly woman I encountered on my first day at work?'

She shrugged a delicate shoulder. 'Do you care?'

'Megsy, of course I care.' He was serious now. She eased back a little more just to be sure. Yes. His brow was furrowed, his lips were in a thin line and his eyes were serious and intent. 'I care very much about you. In fact…' He swallowed, unsure if he was about to make a terrible mistake or not. Even if he was, at that moment he didn't care. He needed to tell her. He felt the timing was right.

He just hoped her response would be the one he'd been dreaming about. 'I'm…er…I'm in love with you, Megan Iris Edwards.'

At his words, Megan felt as though her heart had stopped beating. She blinked, one long steadying blink, and looked at him again. Had he said what she'd just thought he'd said? He l-loved her? No. It couldn't be true. He couldn't…could he?

'It's all right if you don't feel the same way,' he rushed on. 'I didn't mean to push you into anything or to scare you off, for that matter. Hmm. Didn't really think this through did I but, nevertheless, there it is. I'm totally in love with you.' He shook his head and chuckled. 'Can't seem to stop saying it now.'

Megan still looked up at him, watching him, seeing his pleasure in the words he was speaking to her. This wasn't a man who was feeding her a line. Neither was he a man who was saying these words for any work or social gain. He'd been through a bad marriage, had raised a daughter on his own, and now he was telling her that he loved her.

He was an amazing man and she wanted to tell him how she felt, to let him know she accepted this declaration, that she wanted him to hold her in his arms for ever…but no words appeared to be forming on her tongue. Her emotions were so overpowering, so overwhelming that she found it impossible to speak.

Doing the only thing she could think of to do under the circumstances, she grabbed his head and pulled it down so their lips could meet once again. This time, as she kissed him, she put everything she could into the kiss, to let him know how much she loved him in return, to show him just how much he meant to her. She loved him so much more simply because he'd taken a chance, had put himself out on that precipice of love and declared his true feelings.

'Don't go to England,' he whispered against her lips.

'No.' She kissed him again.

'Oi. What's going on in here?' Heather asked as she came back into the kitchen, a beaming smile on her face. 'I go and make one little phone call and the next thing I know you two are playing a game of sucky face.'

'Aye,' her father answered, taking his time in releasing Megan, one arm still placed firmly about her waist. 'And such a good game it is, too.' As though realising his words, he quickly turned and looked at Heather, pointing a finger. 'But not for you to play. Not yet. You're too young. You hear your da'?'

Heather giggled and embraced them both. 'I hear ya, Da', and I couldn't be happier. I think it's totally grand that you two are together. You little beauty.' She spoke the last three words with a perfect Australian accent and both Megan and Loughlin laughed.

'So what now?' she asked, all agitated with excited energy. 'Are you going to get married?' Her big brown eyes were filled with pleading. 'Do I get to be bridesmaid?'

'Whoa, there.' Both adults spoke in unison and Megan released her hold on Loughlin, needing a bit of space. Things were moving way too fast for her and when she chanced a glance at Loughlin, she could see he felt the same way. Although he'd declared his love for her, that didn't mean they were about to do a Strathspey reel down the aisle.

'Usually people try dating first,' Loughlin answered. 'See how well they get along together.'

Heather waved his words away as though they meant nothing. 'We all know you two get along well. The whole town knows it.'

'Well…the whole town is just going to have to wait for us to sort things out in our own time, in our own way, and preferably by ourselves.' Loughlin's words were clear and direct and as he spoke, he saw Megan visibly relax. He took her hand in his and gave it a little squeeze. 'First on the menu, though, is a lovely, healthy breakfast where we can relax and enjoy each other's company. Sound good, Megsy?'

Megan nodded her head slowly, looking from father to daughter and back again. Had Loughlin just implied that they were now dating? Did that mean he was going to be demonstrative of his newly confessed love in public? Could she deal with that?

'Go and get ready to leave, hen,' Loughlin instructed Heather, and when the child had left the room he turned and took Megan's other hand in his. 'Relax. We'll take this as slowly as you like. As slowly as both of us need. Yes?'

'Yes.' She nodded for emphasis. The last thing she wanted him to think was that she *wasn't* interested in dating him. She was. Utterly and completely.

'So…we'll date?'

'Yes.'

'We're dating.' It was as though he needed to convince himself of it as well and as he said the words he let go of one of her hands and pushed his fingers through his hair. 'We're dating! I'm dating someone. I'm dating you. Megan Iris. We're dating!'

'Lochie?' Megan put her hand to his cheek. 'Is this what you want?'

Was it? He loved her. He'd told her he loved her and whilst she hadn't confessed reciprocal feelings, she had kissed him. She wanted to date him. Surely that was a sign that she wasn't going to snatch and jerk his heart all around the wide brown countryside. He knew his own reservations came from the fact that Bonnie had messed him around so badly before, had abused his love for her, using it as leverage whenever she needed it. And he'd let her.

But he'd changed now. It had been nine years since he'd filed for divorce and even though Bonnie had continued to flit in and out of his life, he'd at least taken charge of the situation and done what was best for himself and Heather.

He'd brought his daughter halfway around the world, having no idea he'd find such terrifying happiness. He hadn't expected it. He hadn't asked for it yet he wanted to be with Megan more than he'd wanted anything else in the world. Still…what if she hurt him?

When he looked at her, it was to find concern in her dazzling blue eyes, to find desire and… Was that love? Could it be possible that she *did* feel the same way? Did she love him? He desperately wished for it to be so. 'Do I want to date you?' He leaned into her hand, loving the way it felt to be touched in such a caring way. It was these sorts of little things, the small things in a relationship, that made all the difference and it was these small things that he'd missed the most over the years. Now the woman standing before him, gazing up at him with happiness reflected in her eyes, was offering to fill that void. Why on earth would he be fool enough to knock it back? 'Och, aye, Megsy. I do.'

His words were strong. His eyes were convincing and Megan relaxed a little. As though to prove his words, he brushed a delicate yet promising kiss across her lips. 'If it means I get to kiss you any time I like. If it means I get to hold your hand when we're walking down the street. If it means I can call you day or night and night or day, then you'd better believe I want to date you.'

As he spoke, he punctuated his words with more of those addictive kisses yet when he pulled back and looked at her once more, he saw fear in her eyes. 'What is it?'

Megan opened her mouth to speak but no words came.

'You're not used to being demonstrative in public,' he guessed. Megan nodded. 'That's all right.' He lifted her hands to his lips and kissed them. 'We'll take it slowly. People will talk, to be sure, but it will be nice talk.'

'I know they mean well but it's not only that which concerns me. I can deal with that. But there is something else. It's…it's just that…' She stopped and shook her head.

'What? Come on. You can tell me anything.'

Megan sighed and looked at him. 'Sometimes I feel as though I don't really know you all that well. I mean, I know I like the way you kiss me, the way you make me feel when you hold me close, the way I feel so happy when I'm with you, but there's still so much I don't know. And I want to, Lochie. I want to know the *real* you.

'You have this amazing ability to be able to look at people, to read their expressions, to know what's going on inside them, to understand them,' she continued. 'You're brilliant in the way you help people. It's as though you unlock their psyches and that's an incredible gift to have… But I don't have that gift. I see glimpses, occasionally, of the pain and hurt you've been through but you keep that part of yourself firmly locked away. I understand that, the locking-away part, because that's what you need to do to help you to move forward with your life, but you can't keep it locked away for ever.'

Megan stood on tiptoe and pressed a kiss to both his cheeks, then planted one firmly on his lips. 'I want to get to know you, Loughlin McCloud. The *real* you. Will you let me? *Can* you let me in? Can you trust me?'

It was a defining moment in his life. He knew it. He felt it. He'd been dreading it for years. He'd confessed his love to the woman before him and now she was asking him for the key to his inner sanctum. She was asking him to trust her. To really lay his pain, his hurt and his failures out for her to see.

He swallowed and she watched his Adam's apple slide up and down his smooth neck before meeting his gaze once again.

'I love you, Lochie.' Her words were plain and simple. '*Please* trust me.'

CHAPTER ELEVEN

SHE loved him!

Had she just said that? Did he need to get his hearing checked? Loughlin looked into her eyes and saw that the love was really there—had always been there—but he hadn't been absolutely sure until she'd said the words. He'd felt it in her kiss, he'd experienced it in her tenderness, but to hear her say the actual words made him feel…euphoric. Euphoric and alive!

Loughlin bent and kissed her lips once more, needing to taste her love, and she didn't disappoint him. The euphoria at their mutual declarations remained strong within him but at the same time he could also see the road ahead…a road he still wasn't sure he wanted to traverse.

Yes, he loved Megan but loving a woman in the past had brought him a lot of heartache and pain. Was he ready to really put himself out there again? To open himself up, faults and all, to a woman he admired as much as Megan?

Megan could almost feel the tug of war happening deep within him and decided he needed some space. Smiling up at him, she squeezed his hand. 'Let's go have breakfast together. The three of us. Let's just enjoy being together.'

He nodded slowly. 'That's a good place to start.' He raised her hand to his lips and kissed it. 'And if you don't feel comfortable about me holding your hand or touching you in public, then say so. We both need to be comfortable with this, Megsy.'

'Aye.'

Her answer brought a smile to his lips and it was exactly what she needed. Seeing Loughlin smile helped her to deal with the trepidation in her heart. They'd both declared their love to other people before and both had been hurt. Wariness was second nature and whilst she didn't like it, she accepted that it was part and parcel of the road they were now travelling on. At least they were taking the journey together.

Heather hadn't stopped smiling all the way through breakfast and the fact that the three of them had turned up in the same car had started the rumour mill. Strangely enough, Megan wasn't bothered by it. She'd told Loughlin that she loved him and although she didn't want the pressure from all and sundry, she wasn't going to hide the fact that they were, indeed, a couple.

Love wasn't given to be hidden.

After breakfast, they stopped off at the hospital and did a quick ward round, Loughlin turning on the charm as he chatted with Mrs Newbold.

'There's something different about you this morning, young man,' the woman declared.

'Really? I didn't shave as closely as I usually do.' He turned his head this way and then that. 'Need a new razor,' he confided in a whisper.

'No, that's not it,' Mrs Newbold tutted and turned to look at Megan. 'What do you think it is, young Megan?'

'Uh…well…I…' Megan fumbled, caught a little off guard. It didn't matter, though, Mrs Newbold snapped her old fingers together as though having a moment of clarity.

'Aha! That's it. It's not just my dashing Scotsman who looks different, it's you as well, Dr Edwards.' Mrs Newbold sighed theatrically then nodded firmly. 'It's about time the two of you came to your senses. Anyone could see the two of you were perfect for each other.'

'Then we have your blessing?' Loughlin asked, his words receiving the odd gasp here and there from other members of staff. He'd just confirmed that Mrs Newbold was indeed speaking the truth.

'Without a doubt, laddie.' She held out her hands to both of them and they each took one, receiving a firm squeeze. 'You'll have a long and happy life together.'

'Predictions as well as insight.' Loughlin's grin was encompassing. 'Mrs Newbold, I think we should employ you as the fortune-teller at the next Kiama Fair.'

The old woman laughed and then started to cough. Both doctors ensured she was made as comfortable as possible. Megan checked her oxygen saturations whilst Loughlin monitored her. Soon Mrs Newbold was relaxing back against the pillows, her eyes closed as she rested.

'She doesn't have too much longer,' Loughlin said to Megan as they left the hospital, Heather running ahead of them to her dad's ute.

'Agreed, although I have to say that that's exactly what I thought when I first started working in Kiama and thankfully she's still with us.'

'Let's hope she pulls through this bad bout of infection to continue to stay with us.'

Megan slid her hand into Loughlin's and he looked at her with surprise. 'You really care about these people.' It was a statement. 'I really like that about you, Loughlin.'

'Like? Or love?' He waggled his eyebrows up and down as he spoke.

Megan smiled as he held the car door open for her. 'Love,' she responded, and was rewarded with a delicious butterfly kiss across her lips.

'Honestly? Are you two going to be kissing all the time now?' Heather asked from the back of the ute.

'Aye,' her father responded, his eyes alive with delight. Loughlin drove through the streets of the town and when he stopped the car at a red light, he turned and took Megan's hand in his. 'So…you'll stay in Kiama?'

Megan nodded slowly. 'I'll stay wherever you are,' she promised, her voice laced with the power of love.

'Really?' He seemed surprised.

'Of course. It would be difficult to date if we're on opposite sides of the globe.'

'You'd give up advancing your career for me?'

Megan shook her head. 'I wouldn't have been advancing my career, Lochie. I'm more than happy to stay here in Kiama as their director…if they're still happy for me to remain in the position.'

'I'll *make* sure they do.' He gave her hand a little kiss before putting it back in her lap. 'You're not really a career-woman, are you?'

'No. I enjoy my work, I always have, but now I choose to enjoy my life.'

Loughlin nodded in appreciation, her words echoing his own thoughts. He drove down to the foreshore and after he'd parked they all climbed from the ute. Although it was almost the end of May, the weather wasn't too bad for a walk along the beach. The sea would be starting to get colder from now on but there were already a few locals out paddling, enjoying the nice weather while it lasted. Heather spotted a few of her new school friends so quickly took off her shoes before running along the golden sand to meet them.

Loughlin and Megan walked hand in hand to a pleasant sandy spot and sat down. They were both silent for a while, content to watch the waves ebb and flow, the seagulls flying around to see if anyone had hot chips to feed them. Heather was well within their sight as she laughed and talked with her friends.

'She seems to have fitted in seamlessly,' Megan commented, breaking their silence.

'Aye. She's a very friendly girl.'

'So is her father.'

'I'm hardly a girl, Megsy.'

She laughed. 'You know what I mean.'

He turned and looked at her, his eyes intent, his smile slipping from his face as he looked at her lips for a split second. 'Aye, I do.' He kissed her quickly then dragged in a deep breath. 'I like being able to do that. To hold you and touch you whenever I like.'

'I like that, too.'

'Like or love?' he asked again.

Her smile was slow and meaningful. 'Definitely love.'

'I want to just go on kissing you. It's as though all of my dreams are starting to come true.'

'That's nice.'

'It is, but I know that before we can move on, I need to tell you more about my marriage.'

'Yes. I don't want to force you to talk about it, Lochie, but I need to unders—'

'Shh.' He kissed her again. 'You have every right to know and every right to ask. You love me and I love you and it's only natural that we get past hurts out of the way so that we can really move forward with a clean slate.'

Megan nodded, waiting for him to continue.

'I've told you that my marriage wasn't all that good in the end. To start off with, it was fine. I would work. Bonnie would work. We spent as much time together as possible and life started to progress. I put in long hours at the hospital—as does every doctor—and in the beginning it was OK. She understood…or so she said.

'Then when I missed a dinner party, or was late for the opera, or couldn't make a weekend vacation due to a last-minute change in shifts, her patience started to wear very thin. You see, Bonnie is a perfectionist. It's good for her in a business capacity because she does take the most beautiful photographs but in her personal life it started to become an obsession. The house always needed to be neat and tidy. Appointments had to be met exactly on time and the more I was late, the more it made her angry and upset. In her mind we had to be the perfect couple and we were far from it. She thought the world was going to come to an end if I left my dirty socks lying around the house. I couldn't relax at home. I couldn't unwind at work. Life just seemed to be one big stress pit.'

He looked out at the sea, the white caps on the waves looking choppy as the wind pushed them one way and then the other. It was often how he'd felt. The problem was, he'd never articulated his feelings to another person before. Now he needed to because Megan deserved everything he had to give.

'As I've told you, when she found out she was pregnant with Heather it was almost as though it was the last straw. As far as she was concerned, I'd ruined her life. A child would be messy. It would ruin her figure. She'd have to endure pain to bring it into the world. Her work would suffer and things were just starting to pick up for her.' Loughlin shook his head and looked down at his fingers, which were entwined with Megan's. It was as though it was a symbol of their new life together, their hearts entwining as they got to know each other more, as they had new experiences together.

He looked at Megan and saw reassurance and love in her eyes. It was then he knew he could admit his greatest weakness and she wouldn't hold it against him.

'I loved Bonnie. Even though she would yell and scream and berate me at times, I loved her. I begged her to keep the baby and she reluctantly agreed. Once Heather was born, she started flitting in and out of our lives. Each time I'd be a mess when she left, forcing myself to work harder at making my marriage work. Promising her I'd do anything she wanted if it meant we could stay together as a family.'

'You wanted Heather to have the best. A two-parent family.'

'Aye, but I was so wrong. Three times Bonnie ground her razor-blade stilettos into my heart and three times I let her. Then when Heather was almost three years old she caught a nasty cold. It turned into pneumonia and she spent two terrifying nights in hospital.'

'Oh, Lochie.' Megan looked down the beach where the happy twelve-year-old was running about with her friends. 'That must have been so scary for you.'

'It was. My sisters, my mother, *my* family were there to support me. Bonnie wasn't interested and couldn't be bothered returning from Milan to be by her daughter's side. It was then I realised that Heather didn't need to be raised in a two-parent family—she needed to be raised in a *loving* family.'

'But what about *you*? When did you realise that you didn't need to change who you were to try and fit in with Bonnie's idea of perfection?'

Loughlin smiled at her. 'And you said you didn't have the gift of emotional detection.'

'Ah, I only recognise those symptoms because I've been there. I tried everything I could to be the person Calvin needed me to be and in the end it just wasn't enough.'

'We hurt ourselves in so many ways, jeopardising our true selves in order to win approval from people we *think* matter in our lives.'

Megan nodded at his words. 'We should be more intent on gaining our *own* approval.'

'"Love the skin you're in,"' Loughlin quoted.

Megan laughed and squeezed his hand tighter. 'Exactly. That's what I had to learn to do when I first came to Kiama and you've helped me with that journey. You've helped me to realise that I'm a nice person.'

'More than nice,' he murmured, leaning a little closer and kissing her lips. When he pulled back he looked deeply into her eyes, his tone intent. 'Does hearing about my past make you feel any different about me?'

Megan was stunned. Stunned he should ask her such a question. But she also knew he needed to know the answer. 'Yes.

It makes me love you even more. You're open, you're honest, you're willing to lay your past hurts before me. That speaks volumes, Loughlin.'

'I think we're two of a kind, Megsy.'

'It's a miracle we've found each other.'

'Miracle. Divine intervention.' He shrugged. 'I never knew coming to Australia would bring me so much happiness but it has.' Loughlin looked deeply into her eyes. 'There is only one thing left that concerns me.'

Megan held her breath. 'What's that?'

'Your chest pains. I wish you'd told me about them.'

'How? Most of the time they happened when you were around.'

'Gee, thanks.'

She smiled. 'That's not what I meant. They started years ago because I was putting myself under too much stress. I tried once to talk to Calvin about it—given that he was a cardiologist—but he simply brushed me off, telling me to take a vacation.' She shook her head. 'Then, while I was planning the wedding, they became worse.'

'Didn't your parents or Jasper realise?'

'I didn't want to bother them. Jasper had his own life happening with Jennifer and my parents would only have worried more. They know now, though.'

'So you haven't actually had your heart checked?'

'No. It's just anxiety.'

'You're certain?'

Oh, the man was so totally gorgeous, so caring and attentive. Megan kissed him. 'I'm sure.'

'How? How can you be so sure?'

'Because whenever you talk to me with your delicious accent, the chest pains ease.'

'Really?'

'You relax me, Loughlin.'

'But I thought you said the pains got worse when I was around.'

'They did. I know. Confusing, but moving from Sydney to Kiama has eased them because my stress levels are lower. And when you're around, like now, I can breathe in, filling my lungs completely with no pain whatsoever.'

'Is that true?'

'Yes, my darling Scotsman. It is.'

'So having me around is good for your health.' His words were a statement and he nodded as though making up his mind about something. 'In that case, I think I should stay around for ever.'

'Fine by me.'

'Then you'll marry me?'

Megan's eyes widened in surprise. 'Marry?'

'Not today,' he rushed on. 'Not tomorrow, but when we're both ready. When Heather's ready, too. We need to work a lot of things out, to figure out the logistics of where to live and work and stuff like that, but right here and now, if I can hear you telling me that you'll be mine for ever, I can cope with anything.'

'You don't waste time, do you,' she stated, stunned at his words but elated he'd spoken them. He wanted to marry her! This man, who was so different from Calvin. This man, who had looked into her soul and seen the real person there. The man, who had helped her to climb out of the abyss and into the sunlight. The man, who had stolen her heart but given his in return.

'I need to know, Megsy. What we have between us is intense and real. I've *never* felt this way before and I want you by my side. To be with Heather as well, to become a family in our own right.'

'Two parents?'

'Two *loving* parents.'

'I do love your daughter, Lochie.'

'And…what about giving Heather some brothers and sisters?'

Megan could see him holding his breath, anxiously awaiting her reply. Her smile was wide as she nodded. 'I've waited for so long to have children of my own and I wouldn't want to have them with anyone else but you. Besides, you've done the most brilliant job of raising Heather, I don't need to wonder if you're perfect father material because I already know you are. It's another reason why I love you so much.'

'Ah, Megsy, my darlin'.' He lifted her onto his lap, needing to have her closer than she was. 'You have no idea how happy that makes me.'

'Well…why don't you show me, then?' And he did, taking his time as he tenderly kissed her with all the love in his heart.

'Make me the happiest Scotsman in all of Kiama.'

'You're the only Scotsman in all of Kiama,' she pointed out.

'Shh. I'm proposing.'

'Sorry.'

'Marry me, Megsy. Please?'

'Och, aye,' she remarked, a teasing glint in her eyes.

MEDICAL™

Single titles coming next month

A SPECIAL KIND OF FAMILY
by Marion Lennox

When Dr Erin Carmody crashes her car and is
rescued by GP Dom Spencer, the intense attraction
between them knocks her sideways! As Erin begins
to heal, she realises that she belongs with
this handsome single father and his boys. But will
Dom ever trust that their love is truly real...?

EMERGENCY: WIFE LOST AND FOUND
by Carol Marinelli

Every doctor dreads recognising someone in Casualty,
so when James Morrell has to treat his unconscious
ex-wife Lorna, he's shocked! As she recovers, James
realises he doesn't want Lorna as his patient – he
wants her as his wife, this time forever!

On sale 7th August 2009

2 FREE

BOOKS AND A SURPRISE GIFT!

We would like to take this opportunity to thank you for reading this Mills & Boon® book by offering you the chance to take TWO more specially selected titles from the Medical™ series absolutely FREE! We're also making this offer to introduce you to the benefits of the Mills & Boon® Book Club™—

- ★ **FREE home delivery**
- ★ **FREE gifts and competitions**
- ★ **FREE monthly Newsletter**
- ★ **Exclusive Mills & Boon Book Club offers**
- ★ **Books available before they're in the shops**

Accepting these FREE books and gift places you under no obligation to buy, you may cancel at any time, even after receiving your free shipment. Simply complete your details below and return the entire page to the address below. You don't even need a stamp!

YES! Please send me 2 free Medical books and a surprise gift. I understand that unless you hear from me, I will receive 4 superb new titles every month for just £2.99 each, postage and packing free. I am under no obligation to purchase any books and may cancel my subscription at any time. The free books and gift will be mine to keep in any case.

M9ZED

Ms/Mrs/Miss/Mr ....Initials ....

BLOCK CAPITALS PLEASE

Surname ....

Address ....

....

....Postcode.................................

Send this whole page to to:
UK: FREEPOST CN8I, Croydon, CR9 3WZ